The arrangement was : parents would see him on to the train in London, and Sam's uncle would meet him at the station in Carlisle.

But when Sam rings home to say that he has arrived safely, he isn't telling the whole truth. He has known all along that his uncle won't be there.

He takes a taxi to his uncle's lonely cottage and finds it locked and silent. He settles down to sleep under the stars, and that's when he sees the UFO going over the hill.

When Uncle Black finally turns up, he is badly shocked to see Sam. But why is he so bad-tempered? And what is hidden in the locked room in the cottage?

Sam begins a battle of wits with his uncle, and the discovery of the tiny UFO and its occupants leads Sam and two new friends into an adventure that they – and the world – will never forget.

David Schutte was born in Crouch End, North London. Brain surgeon, pop singer and Olympic athlete are just some of the things he never achieved. Apart from being an author, he is also a specialist children's bookseller. He lives in Hampshire with his wife and children.

Also by David Schutte

The Naitabal Mystery series:

1. DANGER, KEEP OUT!
   (Originally published as MUD PIES AND WATER-BOMBS)

2. WAKE UP, IT'S MIDNIGHT!

3. WILD WOODS, DARK SECRET

4. BEHIND LOCKED DOORS

SKELETONS IN THE ATTIC   (A non-Naitabal prequel
                                          to GHOST ISLAND)
5. GHOST ISLAND

6. DEAD MAN'S CHEST

Non-fiction:

WILLIAM – THE IMMORTAL An illustrated bibliography

DAVID SCHUTTE

SAM AND THE U.F.O.

To SARAH

BEST WISHES

David Schutte

Junior Genius

First published in 2001 by Junior Genius

ISBN 1-904028-07-1

1 3 5 7 9 8 6 4 2

A CIP catalogue record for this book
is available from the British Library

Printed in the U.K. by
Polestar AUP Aberdeen Ltd

TO MARIE

WITH LOVE

Contents

CHAPTER ONE

The Journey

"Are you travelling alone, little boy?"

Sam Johnson lowered his book, *The Galaxy of Doom*, and looked across at the elderly lady opposite. The train was moving out of the station, and the rest of their section was empty. Sam gave an exaggerated glance at the vacant seats.

"Yes," he said.

He raised his book again and continued reading.

"I live in Carlisle," the lady announced. Her voice was high-pitched and penetrating.

Sam, who had read three words, looked up, said "Oh" and read another three words.

"In fact," the lady went on, "I've lived there all my life. Seventy-five years."

Sam didn't reply, but tried desperately to keep his concentration on *The Galaxy of Doom*. He had reached the exciting part where the evil Morgolyphs from Galaxy Ten were transplanting a human brain into *Tyrannosaurus Rex*.

"Did you hear me, little boy?"

"Pardon?" said Sam, irritably.

"I said I've lived there for seventy-five years."

"Gosh," said Sam, without enthusiasm. He wished the Morgolyphs from Galaxy Ten would transplant a gag on to *Tyrannosaurus Mouth*.

"I have five brothers and five sisters," the old lady continued, proudly. "They're all alive."

Sam was surprised they hadn't been bored to death.

"Oh," he mumbled.

She then told him their names and ages, in order, and what

happened to them, and who they married and what their children were doing now. She told him about the people she lived next door to, and who she lived next door to at the house she lived in before that. And every time she told him something, her eyes penetrated his, and if he tried to read, or didn't answer, she asked him if he was listening.

Sam knew the journey from London to Carlisle was going to be long, but he never suspected it would be like a mediaeval torture. At first, he accepted the situation. But as the journey went on, and she started asking questions about *him*, he decided to rebel. Her grey eyes drilled into his, waiting for answers.

"Have you any brothers or sisters?"

"No."

"Any aunts and uncles?"

Sam had lots of aunts and uncles.

"No," he said. He was not normally dishonest, but this week, he knew, he had already embarked on a life of crime. He didn't suppose a white lie to a stranger would make any difference. He was so utterly bored by the old lady's conversation that the only excitement he could generate was by telling a little white lie. All he wanted to do was to finish his book in peace.

But once he had told the first little white lie, of course, the next one became a challenge. The lies that followed became greyer and greyer, until in the end he was telling whopping great big black ones. He discovered quite quickly that the biggest, blackest lies were like a black hole in space – once you had got into them, you couldn't possibly get out again.

"Do you live in a big house, little boy?"

"No," said Sam.

"A small house, then?"

"No."

"A flat?"

"No."

10

"Well, where do you live, then?"

There was a pause.

"In a cave," said Sam.

The lady was shocked.

"Surely not!" she said. "That can't be so, and I think you're not telling me the truth." She wagged a finger at him.

"I am," lied Sam. "I live in a cave with my dad. He's a hermit."

"If your father's a hermit, and you live in a cave, where did you get your nice clothes and suitcase from?" said the lady triumphantly.

"He's a millionaire hermit," said Sam, unabashed. "It's quite a posh cave, really."

The old lady looked at him with disapproval. The first faint humour that had lingered as a result of his 'naughty' fibs had disappeared and was replaced by a grim frown.

"And where is this cave?" she said.

"In the Himalayas," said Sam.

"In the—? Nonsense! *Nonsense!*"

"It is," said Sam. He was just beginning to enjoy the journey for the first time.

"And I suppose your mother lives there, too?"

"No."

The old lady seemed relieved.

"No," Sam went on, "she was never married to Dad anyway. She married a Swedish Prince. They live in Brazil now."

The woman decided to change tack.

"And where are you going after Carlisle? Holidaying with friends in the Lake District?"

"No."

"Who are you staying with, then?"

"No one. I'm staying on my own."

"Oh?" snapped the old lady. "Then why does your luggage say 'Mr and Mrs Jeremy Black, Drift Hill Cottage' as the address? Your name's not Jeremy Black, because you told me two hours ago it was Sam Johnson!"

Sam looked up at her slowly and thought of his Uncle Black. He was a miserable man who hated children. He'd never done a day's work in his life.

"Mr Black is a criminal psychologist," he said. Feeling this wasn't impressive enough, he added, "He's the best one in the country. I'm visiting him to see if he can. . . help me."

The woman shuddered.

"Help you? Help you. . . what?"

"Stop telling lies," said Sam.

"Ah!" The woman didn't exactly smile again, but she looked relieved. "So everything you have told me so far has been big fibs, has it?"

"No," lied Sam. "Everything I've told you has been the truth. That was one of the things Mr Black told me. He said on the journey to Carlisle I should try very hard to tell the truth."

"No wonder your poor mind is in such confusion – living in a cave with a hermit father," murmured the lady.

Shortly afterwards, finally exhausted by the wildness of Sam's claims, she went to sleep. Sam immediately escaped to the opposite end of the train. When he got there he realised, in his rush to escape, he had left his book behind. He couldn't bear the thought of going back in case the old lady woke up and started talking to him again.

At Carlisle station, Sam saw the old lady hanging round, looking for him, asking people if they'd seen him, holding something and pointing. He hid behind a pillar for ten minutes until she had gone.

As he made his way out of the station, he began to have serious qualms about his earlier, bigger, unforgivable crime. He sat down on a bench outside the station, took a creased letter from inside his shirt, and read it once more.

Dear Babs, Henry and Sam,
I'm afraid I won't be able to take Sam after all while
you're both in New York on your business trip. My sister
Anne's been taken ill and I've got to go to Ireland to nurse
her. It might be weeks. Jeremy will be here, but he doesn't
want to be bothered looking after Sam on his own. It's
enough to hope that he'll do some painting and fix the
guttering while I'm away. He keeps promising, but you
know what a grumpy old so-and-so he is at the best of times.
I'm so sorry for the short notice and the disappointment for
Sam. Don't worry, Sam, I'll make it up another time.
Your loving,
Auntie Mabel.

The letter had arrived at home when his parents were out at
work. The envelope had been addressed to "Mr and Mrs
Johnson *and Sam*", so Sam hadn't committed any crime by
opening it. But once he'd read the startling contents, he'd
decided *not to show it to his parents*, and his life of crime
had begun.

All along, there was no chance of Sam going to New York
because of the expense, plus the fact that his parents would
be working the whole time. Instead, he'd had two choices.
He could stay with a boring cousin in a fume-packed part of
London, or he could stay with his Aunt Mabel in the wilds of
Cumbria. He loved wilderness, and he hated cities, so the
choice had been simple. He wanted Cumbria, not the cousin.
But if his parents had seen the letter. . .

That was why he hadn't shown it to them. That was why
there was no one to meet him at the station.

He pushed the letter back into his shirt, then considered the
next problem: before leaving for New York, his parents
were waiting for his telephone call to tell them he'd arrived

13

safely.

He went into a public call box, put his jumper over the mouthpiece and dialled the number.

"Hello, Mum, it's me."

"Pardon? I can hardly hear you. Where are you?"

"Carlisle station," mumbled Sam.

"Did you say Carlisle? Is Uncle there to collect you?"

Sam wanted to avoid a direct lie. "I'm going to the cottage now," he shouted. "Sorry. It's a bad line. I'm going now. Bye!"

"Bye, love. Have a nice holiday. Give our love to Auntie Mabel. See you when we get back from New York."

Sam replaced the receiver and breathed a sigh of relief. He was glad that the trickiest part was over. Now his parents could go on their business trip without worrying about him.

Drift Hill Cottage was fifteen miles away. Sam found a taxi easily enough outside the station. The driver asked a few harmless questions which Sam could answer truthfully. It was a relief not having to make things up.

The journey south along the winding roads and into the great sprawling hills of Cumbria was uneventful. It was eight o'clock in the evening when the taxi came over the brow of yet another hill. The driver pointed to a white and lonely house in the distance, standing on its own way ahead of them and high up to their right.

"That must be Drift Hill Cottage now," he said.

It was three miles since they had left the last village, and they were in the middle of nowhere. Half a mile to the left, in the flat bed of the valley, was a small farmhouse. It seemed to be the cottage's closest neighbour.

The taxi took the right fork off the long straight road, and began to climb the hill. Drift Hill, Sam thought. There was no sign of life as the taxi drew up outside the cottage. A five bar gate hung despondently on its rusty hinges at the left side of the cottage. Sam dismounted, and the driver helped him with his luggage.

"Will you be all right?" said the driver. "The place looks deserted to me."

"If my uncle's not here now, he'll be back soon," said Sam. "He knows I'm coming, anyway." More grey lies.

He paid the taxi driver from the money his father had given him for expenses. Then the taxi did a five point turn in the narrow road and drove off.

There was no door at the front of the cottage, so Sam left his cases where they were. He opened the wide dilapidated gate and went round to the back. He felt sure his Uncle Black would be pleased to see him after all. It might be a nice surprise. He'd always been a grumpy uncle, but he surely wouldn't be as grumpy as all that.

Sam knocked long and hard at the door, but there was no answer. He tried the handle without success, then walked round the house. It looked almost as if no one lived there. Some of the paint-work was peeling, and one piece of guttering had come loose and was hanging down at a dangerous angle. All the windows were locked. He looked into the little kitchen, but could see no signs of food or recent habitation. Then he went round to the front again. There was the board saying 'DRIFT HILL COTTAGE'. He looked in at the windows. One room was a little sitting-room with just two armchairs. The other room had curtains drawn across. Sam rapped on the window of the curtained room, thinking that his uncle might have gone to sleep. There was still no response.

Sam didn't quite know what to do next. He had been prepared for a telling-off from his grouchy Uncle Black, but now he wasn't there, Sam felt disappointed. Then he felt a sudden thump of his heart. Perhaps his uncle had gone to Ireland as well! What would he do then?

Luckily, the evening was warm, and there was no sign of

rain. He sat on his suitcase for the next hour, watching the road. Now and again a car appeared over the distant brow of the hill, or from the opposite direction along the straight. As each one came into view he wondered if it contained his Uncle Black, and if it would turn up the little lane. But none did.

At nine-thirty it began to get a little darker. Sam started looking round the house to see where he could sleep if he was locked out all night. The only outbuilding was an old stone structure that had been lime-washed inside and out. It looked as if it had been useful once – a long time ago. It was littered with rusty tins and tools, rotting bags of garden chemicals, and a lot of dust and cobwebs. Sam decided he would rather sleep under the stars than in there.

It grew darker and darker. Still there was no sign of his uncle. Sam had some chocolate and biscuits in his rucksack, and he sat in the grass with his back against a fence, finishing them up.

Before long, he started to feel chilly. He began to look longingly at the bright lights of the little farmhouse down in the valley, half a mile away. The ground in between was dark now, perhaps even boggy. If he went by road it would be even further.

He decided to stay and wait for his uncle's return.

He had brought a sleeping-bag in his luggage in case he wanted to sleep out one night. He hadn't imagined for one moment that it would be the night of his arrival – perhaps *every* night if his uncle didn't show up. He decided to get into it with all his clothes on. He had already discovered a patch of long, soft grass. He formed his luggage into three sides of a miniature rectangle, rolled up two jumpers into a pillow, climbed into the sleeping-bag, and settled down into the snug little space. He lay on his back looking up at the stars.

He had never really looked at the stars in the countryside

before. In London, the sky was always yellow from the street lights. Here in Cumbria the sky was deep and black from one horizon to the other. The milky way was splashed across it in a glorious arch of a hundred billion stars. Sam gazed at it in awe.

After a few minutes, he saw his first satellite. At first he thought it was a shooting star. It travelled straight across the night sky as a fast-moving point of constant light, only fading as it moved towards the distant hills. Once he had seen one, and worked out what it was, he saw several more. He found that he could spot them more easily by fixing his eyes on a single star. That way he could detect any movement in the sky over quite a large area. As soon as he noticed something he could turn to look at it directly and see what it was.

After twenty minutes he *did* see a shooting star. It suddenly sparkled brilliantly way off to the west. He turned his head only just in time to see it properly. It faded and disappeared in less than a second – a tiny meteor no bigger than a grain of sand. It was travelling as fast as fifty miles every second, burning out in the atmosphere perhaps fifty miles above him. Sam knew that thousands of millions of meteors entered the Earth's atmosphere every day. Only a few burned out with enough light to be visible to the naked eye.

Soon, he began to feel drowsy. There was no sign of a vehicle arriving. The cottage stood blacker than the sky, a cold and impenetrable fortress. Sam had grown used to the idea of sleeping under the stars. He began to hope that his uncle wouldn't return that night after all.

What made Sam wide awake again was another shooting star – except that it *wasn't* a shooting star. It came from the south west, and it was glowing with a brilliant pink light. At first Sam thought it must be an aeroplane. But it was coming lower and lower, bending slowly towards the earth. It seemed as if it was coming straight towards Drift Hill, and as it approached it was getting faster and brighter. When it was overhead it suddenly flared in a blinding spark, then returned to its former brilliance.

Sam jumped up, still in his sleeping-bag. He watched the object for another five seconds or so before it dropped beyond the back of the field behind Drift Hill.

Sam knew it was something different, but he didn't know what. Perhaps it was a small meteorite. Perhaps – his mind raced back to *The Galaxy of Doom* – perhaps it was a spaceship. . . a *real* spaceship. The thought of it set his heart bumping. He wanted it to be a real spaceship more than anything else in the world.

He looked at the black silhouettes of the wind-bent trees that crowded the dark horizon of the hill. He tried to use them to memorise the path the object had taken. He would go in that direction in the morning, to look for signs of anything that might have come down.

He remained alert and excited for a time, watching the sky for a little while longer.

Soon, he was fast asleep. He didn't hear the tiny sound in the garden, a few minutes later, only twenty feet away.

CHAPTER TWO

The Zargans

At the same time when Sam was travelling in his taxi from Carlisle station, a spaceship was travelling somewhere between the stars. Sam's journey had lasted half an hour. So far, the spaceship's journey had lasted for *five thousand years*.

The maximum speed of the taxi had been sixty miles an hour, but the spaceship had reached ninety-three thousand miles a *second*, which is half the speed of light. It had been slowing down, now, for almost six months of our time. Its current velocity was only a hundred and twenty thousand miles an hour, which was still two thousand times faster than the taxi.

When Sam was arranging his sleeping-bag on the grass, the spacecraft was penetrating a solar system, the two hundred and fortieth that it had encountered so far on its long, long journey. It was approaching the night side of a planet that lay directly in its path. Fifty thousand miles ahead, the lights of a thousand cities were glowing like the countless tiny stars of another distant galaxy.

Inside its cabin, the bio-panel was the only light that shone in the blackness of the spaceship. Three sets of eyes watched the flickering bio-computers which monitored their approach. Beyond the screens, through a window of pure diamond, they watched the growing mass of the light-encrusted world that slowly approached them.

"There is no doubt," said Zambel, "that this planet is inhabited. Look at the lights – thousands of them. Those are cities. For every city there may be a million intelligent beings."

"I wonder what are our chances," said Lam, "of surviving against such odds?"

The third crew member, Mogon, pointed towards the bio-crystal display.

"We have only ninety seconds in which to decide," he said calmly. "After that, we lose our chance to inject into orbit around the planet. If we delay longer, and then decide not to orbit, our course will have been altered by the planet's gravity."

"What does the bio-computer tell us about the planet?"

"Only, so far, that it seems hospitable."

"At least if we drop into orbit," argued Lam, "we will have more time before we decide to attempt a landing."

"And the longer we're in orbit," countered Zambel, "the more chance we will have of being detected by their instruments. Assuming that they are advanced enough for that."

"They certainly are, Zambel," said Mogon. "Our equipment confirms the presence of artificial satellites in this area."

"How is the language analyser behaving?"

"We have absorbed a great deal of radio transmission from the planet. The analyser is still working on the data. It may take quite a while before it can make any sense of it."

"How long have we now?"

"Sixty seconds."

"Then we have no choice. We must enter orbit, then land as quickly as possible after that. We all know the situation: if we can't find our supply of gold catalyst here, the next planetary system is over four light-years away. We have barely enough catalyst to keep us going for two light-years. We have travelled a long way. We must not fail now. We owe it to Zarg, we owe it to our distant ancestors, and we owe it to those more recent ones who have brought us thus far in safety and comfort. At all costs, we must protect our precious cargo."

"We also need copper to repair the secondary drive accelerator," Mogon reminded them. "We can probably manage without it, but I for one would feel much happier with it repaired. If it should fail altogether, it would seriously increase our journey time, and possibly put us in the same gold shortage situation again at some time in the future."

"We have no choice," repeated Zambel. He waved his hand across a pulse pad, and the bio-computer responded with a warning crystal light.

"Firing in thirty seconds," said Lam.

As they swung into the planet's gravitational pull, they began to enter its sunrise. For a few seconds the edge of the huge sphere below them became a glowing iridescent arc as the light from its hidden sun was refracted through the edge of the atmosphere.

"Please apply your safety harnesses," said Lam. "Full power retro ignition in fifteen seconds."

All three of them had reached their couches and were now fastening their straps. From their new positions they could still observe the bio-display and the planet. They could also communicate via the pulse pad if necessary, but this would become more difficult under the force of deceleration.

"Five seconds."

As the tremendous retro force was applied, their months of normal weight came to an end. They were suddenly crushed by the power of several gravities as the nuclear motors applied thrust of huge intensity to bring the ship into a high orbit. By coincidence, the planet's sun had been eclipsed by the planet as they approached. Now it appeared, climbing slowly from their right, its rays spreading further and further into the atmosphere of the planet's dawn. As the intense retro drive pressed them into their seats, they had their first glimpse of the beautiful jewel blossoming beneath them. It was like a flower unfolding its petals to the sun. It was blue, brown and white – a glittering gem set in the black velvet cloth of endless space.

Before the increasing G-force overcame his power of speech, Mogon said: "I wonder if its inhabitants are as beautiful as the planet. . ."

Safely in orbit around the planet, the three travellers were busy enquiring on the APDCS (Automatic Planetary Data Collection System) and reading off statistical information.

"Initial calculations indicate," said Lam, "that the length of the day on this planet is equivalent to twenty of our days back home."

"This planet is small compared with several of the others in this system, but it's still a giant," said Mogon. "The diameter is over twenty-five million kilometres."

"The atmosphere is twenty-one per cent oxygen – much richer than the air on Zarg – with a small amount of carbon dioxide. There are traces of inert gases, but mostly nitrogen, as we might expect."

"Seventy-one per cent of the planet is covered by water, twenty-nine per cent by land. Of the land surface area, only two narrow bands in the northern and southern hemispheres provide temperate conditions that would suit us. The two poles are well below the freezing point of water, and much of the equatorial zone has sparse vegetation. Apart from that, vegetation is plentiful."

Mogon regarded his two companions.

"Then there seems to be no reason why we should not continue our descent to the surface of this planet and restock our gold supplies."

"Agreed. As you pointed out, we have even less choice now than we had before," said Zambel.

"I would suggest," Mogon continued, "that we land in the

northern temperate zone on the night side of the planet. Although a night landing can make it more dangerous for us to find our bearings, it may be much more hazardous to land on an inhabited planet in daylight. At least this way we shall have a chance of concealing ourselves and our ship before any intelligent beings become too curious."

"It will be unfortunate if they are creatures of nocturnal habit," said Lam. "We would then be at a double disadvantage."

"The chances of the dominant species being nocturnal, in our ancestors' experience, is a slim one. Let us ask the bio-computer to recommend possible trajectories to get us down. We have vital work to do."

They felt as if they were careering down a rough Zargan mountain in a flimsy box. The spaceship bumped and yawed, bouncing and skidding through the upper layers of the atmosphere. They could see nothing through the windows except the red bouquet of hot gases that streamed from the nose of the rocket.

At first, as they descended, the temperature inside the cabin increased. This was expected. But as time went on, the whole spacecraft began to overheat alarmingly.

"This is not good," said Lam, with difficulty. They were not only getting too hot, but the pressure of deceleration was still almost unbearable. "We are still three hundred thousand kilometres above the surface. There must be something wrong."

With a huge effort, Mogon turned his head to look at the bio-display.

"The mother ship and our cargo are at normal temperature," he said. "They are correctly insulated. It's only we who are overheating."

"Yes," said Lam, "and I can see why."

"What is it?" said Zambel.

23

"One set of bolts attaching us to the mother ship have been withdrawn. A malfunction in the undocking system. Hot gases are licking the unprotected side of our command capsule and heating it up."

"Set the bio-computer," said Zambel straightaway, "to eject us if all three of us become unconscious."

"Yes," said Lam, "that is sensible. If we have not solved the problem by then, that will be the moment at which we should part from the mother ship."

"Free of the mother ship," Mogon reminded them, "our heat shield will automatically orientate. Would it not be safer to separate now?"

"No," said Zambel. "Separation means the loss of the main bio-computer facilities and main power unit. We must avoid that option if possible. Early separation could leave us hundreds – or thousands – of kilometres from the mother ship on landing. We would have great difficulties in getting the two units together again."

Once Lam had set the ejection option, he confirmed that he was unable to re-align the docking bolts. There was nothing more that any of them could do but wait. There was no further conversation except the monotonous reports from Lam of cabin temperature and height above the planet. The inside of the cabin grew more and more unbearable.

Eventually, Lam's reports grew fainter, more spasmodic, and finally stopped. In his semiconscious state, Zambel realised that Lam had lost consciousness altogether. He took over reading the display.

Ironically, the craft was only forty seconds from touchdown when Mogon and Zambel, too, lost consciousness. Zambel had realised in his final delirium that ejection was not necessary, but was physically too weak to change the bio-computer's command.

The craft was travelling at half the speed of sound when the landing retro drive ignited. The bio-computer did its duty faultlessly: within two seconds of their unconsciousness there was a small explosion as the cabin section was ejected to one side. The travellers and their mother ship were separated. Three seconds later, the command module had orientated its heat shield, and only thirty-eight seconds after that, the mother craft had landed safely, undamaged. Another five minutes passed before the command module, with its unconscious crew, touched down.

In our terms, the mother ship and its command module were separated by six kilometres. In the Zargan's language, and from their point of view, the distance was twelve thousand kilometres. For a Zargan is only one millimetre high – two thousand times smaller than a human being.

To these tiny aliens, the planet on which they had landed was twenty-five million kilometres across.

It was the Earth.

CHAPTER THREE

The Ants

"Look! There's someone asleep in the garden!"

It was the voice of a girl, shrill with amusement, that penetrated Sam's dream and made him wake up. At first he couldn't remember where he was. But when he opened his eyes to the blinding summer sky, he knew soon enough.

"What's he doing *there*?" said another voice, a little boy's this time. *"Look! He's waking up!"*

Sam hauled himself on to one elbow and blinked towards the voices. He could make out a girl, roughly his own age, long-haired and slim, and a boy, much younger, plump and fair. They were both grinning like chimpanzees and the boy was jumping up and down.

"Hello," said Sam. "Have I overslept? What time is it?"

"Do you *always* sleep in the garden?" said the girl.

"Only when I get locked out," said Sam.

"Why did you get locked out?" said the boy. "Did you do something *bad*?"

"No," said Sam. He *had* done something bad, of course, but it seemed much simpler to tell another lie.

The girl came slowly towards him, the boy in tow.

"Are you supposed to be staying with *him*?" she said, cocking a thumb towards the cottage.

"Old Shoutbum," said the boy. He was hushed by his companion. "Well, he's always shouting at us," he went on. "Whatever we're doing, he always shouts. Doesn't he, Sis?"

"Yes, but I've told you before not to call him Shoutbum – it's rude."

"Sorry."

While this exchange was going on, Sam had extricated himself from the sleeping-bag. He was standing now, clothed but creased, inside his little rectangle of luggage.

"Did he *throw* you out?" asked the girl.

"Oh, no, nothing like that," said Sam. "I'm supposed to be staying here for three weeks. But when I arrived last night there was no one at home. It was a nice night, so I thought I'd rather sleep outside than in that dusty old shed."

"He's back now," said the girl. "His car's outside."

"He must have come back late, then," said Sam, sounding slightly relieved. "But I don't care. It was much more fun sleeping out."

"I wish I could sleep out," the girl said wistfully. "My name's Helen. What's yours?"

"Sam."

"This is my little brother Jimmy. He's six. I'm eleven."

"I'm eleven as well."

"We live at the farm down there." Helen pointed across the valley, then turned to face him, her face glowing with excitement. "Did you see it last night? You must have seen it if you were sleeping out. It came right over here."

"Is it a *flying* farm, then?" said Sam, grinning.

"Not the farm, silly! The UFO!"

"Oh! The UFO! Of course!" Sam had genuinely forgotten about the strange shining object in the sky, and might have thought he'd dreamt it, but for Helen. "You bet I saw it! I was flat on my back watching the sky for nearly an hour. It went over about eleven o'clock."

"Our bedroom faces this way," said Helen. "We always look out towards the road and watch the stars."

"We have our window open sometimes," said Jimmy.

"We saw the UFO go over the hill behind your cottage. That's why we've come up here this morning."

"We're trying to find it," said Jimmy, making the situation absolutely clear.

27

Sam found himself smiling.

"Come on!" he said. "We'll go and look for it together!" He glanced back at the cottage. It stood as quiet and uninviting as it had done the previous evening. "There's no point in hammering on the door and waking him up. I stayed with him and my aunt once before – where they used to live." He dropped his voice to a whisper. "He doesn't get up until midday, sometimes."

"He might shout at us," said Jimmy, summing up.

"Come on!" called Helen, moving off.

With this encouragement, Sam followed them over the wooden fence, and the threesome made its way up the field and over the brow of the hill. Secretly, neither Sam nor Helen had any real hope of finding anything. Sam felt that whatever it was had fallen several miles away. They would never find it within easy walking distance.

Despite their doubts, they made a thorough a search of the local area, at least as much as could be expected in two hours. They found nothing, of course, and it was only the lure of breakfast that made them turn their steps back towards Drift Hill.

Helen and Jimmy waved goodbye and promised to call again.

Sam contemplated the meeting with his uncle with growing trepidation. For the first time he began to realise what a stupid thing he'd done. His uncle was a moody man at the best of times, and extremely lazy. What would he do when he found he'd got Sam to look after? Especially when he thought he was having a few weeks of freedom with his wife gone away? Sam felt more and more horrified at the thought of what he'd done.

He rehearsed his own side of the conversation.

"But they didn't get any letter. . . It was all arranged. . . Mum said it was all okay for me to stay. They didn't know Aunt Mabel had gone away. They didn't get a letter, honest.

I thought it was funny when you weren't at the station to collect me. If you'd had a telephone, I would have called. I had to get a taxi. . ."

There was still no sign of movement in the house. The last thing Sam wanted to do was to wake his Uncle Black prematurely. It might put him in an even worse temper.

Sam sat on an upturned suitcase and started thinking about food. He might be sitting on his suitcase half the day if his uncle was as lazy as he remembered. He suddenly felt envious of his two new friends. They'd be tucking into a delicious farmhouse cooked breakfast by now.

Sam waited another half an hour, which seemed like half a day. Then, quite suddenly, the back door of the cottage opened, and a man came out. Sam recognised his Uncle Black straight away. He was unshaven, his hair hadn't been combed, and he was wearing a grubby white shirt without a collar. His baggy brown trousers were creased and stained and held up with braces. His uncle didn't look across the garden, so didn't see Sam. He had turned towards the side gate and was unlatching it before Sam had time to realise what was happening. Sam shouted.

"Hey! Uncle! It's me, Sam!"

His uncle turned towards the voice, and the colour drained from his face. There was certainly no sign of welcome, only deep shock. When he had recovered slightly, his brow clouded with anger and confusion. He looked briefly at Sam then, still fuming, said in his gruff voice, "What the devil are you doing here?" and accelerated through the gate at twice his previous speed.

Sam, hurt and puzzled, ran after him. But as he rounded the corner of the cottage he heard the sound of an engine being started and the squeal and rattle of a departing car. By the time he reached the gate, the shabby old yellow Ford was already in the distance, turning on to the main road towards the village in a haze of blue smoke.

"Well!" said Sam aloud. He'd expected his uncle to be surprised at his visit – shocked, even – but not hostile. His uncle had always been off-hand, but now he seemed much, much worse. Why had he been so shocked at seeing Sam? He remembered the look in his uncle's eyes, staring at Sam as if he'd seen a ghost. . .

Sam wondered how such a nice, kind woman as his Aunt Mabel could have married such a horrible specimen.

As he stood watching the blue smoke slowly drift away, Sam felt renewed pangs of guilt and horror at what he had done. He'd lied to his parents – a stupid idea at the best of times. Now it meant more complications than Sam had imagined. It was obvious his uncle didn't want him there, and now his uncle would be cross for three weeks and then report him to his parents.

Sam suddenly felt isolated. There was no one else to turn to. All he could hope was that his uncle's anger, when it came, wouldn't be too terrible. Perhaps he'd even make him feel welcome.

Sam shrugged the problem away, and spent the next five minutes looking round the cottage again. The curtained window downstairs was still curtained, and all the doors and windows were still locked. He guessed that his uncle had gone to the village for food and would be back in fifteen or twenty minutes. If he wasn't back by then, Sam would walk down to the farm, explain his plight, and ask for some breakfast.

He moved his luggage to the back door and sat on the big suitcase again. Fifteen minutes passed. Eventually he heard the rattle of a car ascending the hill to the cottage and skidding to a stop. A door banged, and his Uncle Black came slouching round the corner. He was carrying two bottles of milk and two loaves of bread. He stopped and glared at Sam.

"Well, I never," he said. "It's the boy who shouts 'Hey!'

at people. Don't you know it's bad manners to shout 'Hey!'? Didn't that sister of Mabel's teach you any manners, or what?"

It was Sam's turn to be shocked, and he couldn't think of an answer.

"Well?" said Uncle Black. "I just asked you a question. Don't you know it's bad manners not to speak when someone talks to you? You must be the worst-mannered little brat in the country. I can see I'll have to talk with your mother."

"Is there any food, please?" said Sam in a weak voice. "I haven't eaten anything since tea-time yesterday."

"I see. No apology. Just think of your belly straight away," his uncle sneered. "Typical."

Sam glanced up at the dirty, black, stubbled chin. For one moment he met the cold, grey eyes that were despising him. He felt that his uncle had gone quite mad since he had stayed with him last, and again he wondered why. It seemed that he was going to pay a high price for the three weeks of freedom that he had engineered by lying to his parents.

"No answer to that, either, eh?" Uncle Black went on. "Suit yourself." He suddenly thrust the groceries towards Sam. Sam caught hold of the two bottles and one loaf, but the other loaf slipped off the top and fell to the ground.

"Clumsy little idiot," said Uncle Black. "You'd better pick it up and come inside before you drop anything else."

Sam, hurt by the feeling of injustice, picked up the stray bread and followed his uncle into the dim little kitchen. He unloaded the shopping on to a wooden table.

"Now sit down," said Uncle Black.

Sam sat down.

"Let's just get a few things straight," said his uncle. He stood over him. "You're not supposed to be here. Your aunt Mabel wrote a letter saying not to come. Didn't you get it?"

"No." A dirty black lie.

"She's gone to Ireland to look after her sister. I can't have you here. It's too inconvenient. You'll have to go back home."

"I can't go home. Mum and Dad have gone abroad."

"Aren't there any friends you can stay with?"

"No. That's why they arranged for me to stay with you and Auntie Mabel."

His uncle seemed to mellow slightly. He stared at Sam for a few moments longer, calculating.

"All right," he said at last. "But listen. I don't want to see you much. Understand?"

"Yes," said Sam, quietly. It suited him. He didn't want to see much of Uncle Black, either, if he was going to be in a bad temper all the time. He just wanted to be in the glorious fresh air and the untamed hills, not stuffy London.

"I've got things to do, see?" his uncle went on. "Business things. And I don't want you interfering or nosing around. Understand?"

"Yes," said Sam. He made a decision straight away to nose around as much as he could. People who didn't want people nosing around were usually trying to hide something.

"There'll be food in here." His uncle was indicating the kitchen. "You'll have to look after yourself. I'm not cooking for you. You know how to use a cooker, don't you?"

"Yes," said Sam.

"Sometimes I might be away for a day or two. But there'll always be enough food. Understand?"

Sam nodded.

"And the less I see of you, the better. Just keep out of my way, and you'll be all right. Keep out of my way, and maybe I won't have to talk to your mother about your manners. Okay?"

"Yes," said Sam. He knew his mother would only laugh about his manners, anyway.

"You can have the first room at the top of the stairs. There's a key to the back door hanging on that hook" – he pointed – "and you're only allowed in the kitchen, the bathroom, and your own room – right?"

Without waiting for an answer, Uncle Black suddenly went upstairs, and Sam heard a door bang. He pushed the back door key into his pocket, then set about getting himself some breakfast.

Sam's room was at the front of the house. It was only just big enough for the single bed, the chair, and the little chest of drawers.

While he was unpacking, he heard the back door slam. He went to the window and watched his uncle getting into his car and driving off. Sam hoped he'd be gone all day.

From the window he could easily see the farm. Soon after his uncle's car had gone, he saw Helen and Jimmy come out of the farmhouse. They started walking across the coarse grass of the fell towards the cottage. Sam quickly put on some jeans and an old sweater and went down towards the long straight road to meet them.

"Hi!" Sam waved.

Helen and Jimmy waved back and together they walked back up to the cottage.

"My uncle's gone out," said Sam. "He's been really horrible – he's never been like that before. He doesn't want me around. I think it's because he's trying to hide something."

"Why do you think that?" said Helen.

Sam told them the story of his brief confrontation with Uncle Black.

"What are you going to do?" said Helen.

"I want to look round the house," said Sam. "But I need a look-out in case he comes back. Would you mind helping me?"

"Jimmy can do that, he'll be good."

"I'll be look-out," said Jimmy. "You have to shout when someone's coming, don't you?"

"That's right, Jimmy," said Helen. "Good boy."

"We've got to stand him where he can see as far up the road as possible," said Sam. They were climbing the steep hill below the cottage now. "How about on top of the wall?"

Sam indicated the dry stone wall that ran along the top of the fell. It ended on the opposite side of the road, to the right of the cottage. Jimmy climbed to the top. He had a good view of the road to the village for at least half a mile, perhaps more. In the other direction he could see along the straight road all the way to the horizon.

"You know what Mr Black's car looks like, don't you, Jimmy?" said Helen.

"Yes, it's yellow," said Jimmy.

"And you know what it *looks* like?"

"Yes. It's got a black roof and it's rusty."

"Good. Now if you see Mr Black's car coming – *as soon as you see it coming* – you jump off the wall and bang on the front window! Okay?"

"All right."

"And *don't forget, and don't start thinking about something else*, and *don't take your eyes off the road*. Right?"

"All right."

"He's good, really," Helen said to Sam as they both ran round to the back of the cottage. "He won't mess it up. He's done it for me once before."

Sam didn't ask Helen why he'd done it for her once before. He wondered if she'd tell him, but she didn't.

He took out his key and opened the back door of the cottage and they went inside. Apart from the kitchen and a toilet, there were only two rooms downstairs. One was not locked, and contained the two armchairs that Sam had seen through the window the evening before. There were a few odd pieces of uninteresting furniture, a television, a bookcase, and nothing much else. Sam tried the handle of the other room, but it was locked.

"That's the room with the curtains closed," said Sam. He tried the handle again to make sure it wasn't just stiff. "I wonder how we can get in?"

"Let's look upstairs first," said Helen.

"Okay."

There were only two rooms upstairs, plus the bathroom. Sam's room was tiny, but the one where his aunt and uncle slept was much larger. The double bed had not been made and there was a stale smell inside. There was a dressing table and a big wardrobe. A few pieces of clothing were scattered round the floor. They noticed three unwashed coffee cups, several paperback books, and a lot of newspapers.

"He's lazy," Sam whispered, apologising. "It's not like this when Aunt Mabel's here. Anyway, I can't see anything. Whatever he's hiding must be in that room downstairs."

As he said it there was a loud rapping on the window downstairs. It made them both jump. Panic-stricken, they dashed from the room. Making sure they closed the door behind them, they flew down the stairs and outside. Jimmy, showing good sense, had come round the back as well.

"Did he see you?" said Helen.

"No," said Jimmy. "He just came over the hill and I ran."

"Good boy!"

"Now we'd better look scarce," said Sam. "Let's hide round the back of the outbuilding. When he's gone into the cottage we can go somewhere else."

"Down to our house, if you like," said Helen. "There's lots of things to do down there. Or we could go exploring."

They all heard the sound of the car arriving, and had plenty of time to crouch behind the outbuilding. They looked through the window at the back and out through the open door on the opposite side. They watched Sam's uncle come round the corner.

"Red ants!" said Jimmy suddenly.

"Ssshhh!"

Uncle Black stopped and glanced in their direction.

"There's one on my leg!" said Jimmy. He said it in a quieter voice, but it still had suppressed panic in it.

"Well, knock it off, stupid!" hissed Helen. "Ssshhh!"

The last because Uncle Black had decided to walk over to the outbuilding to investigate. When they saw him coming, they ducked down so that he wouldn't see them through the dirty window. They hoped he hadn't seen them already. His footsteps paused in the doorway on the far side, then shuffled and went away again. The door of the cottage opened and closed. The danger had passed.

"You nearly got us caught because of a stupid little red ant!" Helen hissed again at her little brother.

But Jimmy had decided not to stay there any longer. He immediately jumped away. At the same time he was frantically brushing his leg and turning it this way and that, checking for further marauders.

"'S'not just one," said Jimmy, upset by his sister's heartlessness. "There's a whole nest of 'em."

Helen and Sam looked down to where he had been standing.

"You've killed about a hundred of them with your big feet," said Helen.

"I haven't got big feet."

"You have to an ant."

Sam, who had only given the ants a cursory glance at first, suddenly found himself looking at them more carefully. It was true that there were a lot of dead ones, but they hadn't been trodden on.

"That's funny," he said.

"What?"

"Those ants. Jimmy wasn't standing on the concrete ledge – he was standing in the grass. Those dead ants haven't been trodden on – they're not squashed flat."

Suddenly their interest was completely diverted to the red ants. They gathered round the place where Jimmy had been standing and looked where the nest – the heap of earth in the grass – had been disturbed. They could see scores of ants running around the stricken area. But in amongst the grass, and on the little concrete ledge that formed part of the foundation for the outbuilding, there were literally hundreds of dead ants. None of them could remember seeing anything like it before.

"They're just dead," said Sam. "They haven't been squashed. There are more dead ones than live ones, as well. What on earth can be wrong with them?"

"Perhaps they've been poisoned," Helen suggested.

"No," said Sam. "The nest has been disturbed, and something is making them die. Poison wouldn't work like that when a nest is disturbed."

"Unless the grass has been sprayed with poison, and they die as they come out and taste it."

"Don't lick your fingers, Jimmy, just in case," said Sam.

They were still watching closely when an ant climbed up the concrete lip. It ran frantically round, sometimes stopping at a dead companion for a few seconds and then moving on again in its seemingly haphazard fashion. Then, quite suddenly, it collapsed in its tracks and lay still.

Sam and Helen frowned and looked more closely, then looked at each other.

"Did you see that?"

"That's not poison," said Sam.

"It did touch the other ant, though."

"Yes, but—"

"I saw it," Jimmy announced.

Helen ignored him and brightened.

"We've got an old microscope at home!" she said.

"Really?"

"Why don't we look at one under that, and do a post mortem?"

"Good idea!" said Sam.

"Let's find something to put them in."

Suddenly, Uncle Black was forgotten. In their excitement, no one seemed to care whether he came out and told them off, or not. All that mattered was solving the mystery of the ants. They hunted around inside the shed and found an empty seed packet. They carefully scooped several of the tiny dead bodies into it, then walked slowly down the fell to Helen's parents' farm.

CHAPTER FOUR

The Giants

When dawn spread its new light on the Zargan control capsule, the three occupants had already recovered consciousness. They had carried out a series of tests to check that there was no damage to themselves or their craft.

"We have landed safely," Zambel said. He was dictating into the black box mission recorder, and he was looking out through a pane of diamond at the half-lit greenish world that surrounded them. "But we are now detached from the mother ship. A fault developed in the docking bolts of the command capsule. Our attempts to stay with the mother ship were foiled when the heat of re-entry became too intense. All three commanders lost consciousness. We are now without the full power and resources of the mother ship. Its location signal tells us that the mother ship lies in a direction thirty-two degrees east of the planet's magnetic north, approximately thirteen thousand kilometres away. We have every confidence that it is undamaged, and its cargo unharmed.

"Because of damage caused by the emergency, our command capsule cannot fly. If we are to continue our mission we must locate the mother ship on foot, then fly it back to the command capsule. We believe that this task is difficult, but not impossible. It depends largely on the hostility, or otherwise, of the life-forms on this planet.

"The main problem appears to be one of scale. The planet is a giant – twenty-five million kilometres in diameter. It is capable of sustaining Zargankind, but unfortunately is already inhabited by intelligent life. The evidence for this has been our observation of huge lighted cities, visible from thousands of kilometres above the planet as we approached; from the emission of radio signals; and from the presence of artificial satellites.

"Looking through our ports," Zambel continued, "it would appear that we have landed in a dense jungle. The trees themselves have no distinct trunks. They rise out of long, round, grooved stems that are yellow-brown in colour, gradually becoming flatter and greener towards the tops of the plants. Unfortunately, our angle of view means that we are unable to see the top of any tree adjacent to the module.

"Having made our final checks on the external conditions, we are satisfied that it is safe for us to make our first exploration."

Zambel switched the recorder to 'remote' and placed a portable transmitter in a pocket of his protective armour. He and Lam were to make the initial reconnaissance, leaving Mogon in the capsule to monitor their progress.

The first problem was choosing an exit. The capsule was lying at a slight angle in what – to the Zargans – was a huge mound of dust and boulders. Out of the mound grew a jungle of giant shoots. They chose the air-lock that had the shortest drop to the ground, and were soon standing on great knobs of uneven material.

"Now that we are outside," Zambel said into his transmitter, "we can see that the capsule is lying in a dense jungle of blade-trees on a slope of very rough, bare terrain. We can now estimate that the height of the blade-trees is around two or three hundred *metres* – far larger than any trees on Zarg."

"There are many cave entrances in the boulders," Lam contributed, "and I do not like the look of them. They are not natural formations. My fear is that they have been made by a living creature of enormous proportions."

Keeping close together, Zambel and Lam started down the

slope, picking their way carefully over the big boulders of soil that were scattered amongst the blade-trees. Their progress was slow. Zambel spoke into his transmitter with a running commentary to give the black box – and Mogon – as much information as possible about their surroundings.

They clambered from tree to tree, down and down the slope. At length the trees appeared to grow more in clusters, growing out at angles from central roots. As they passed yet another clump, quite green by now, they suddenly stopped.

"Look!" said Lam.

Neither of them could very well help looking: for right in front of them, rising straight out of the rough ground, was a vertical cliff. In their terms, it was two hundred metres high. It was very rough in texture, but of extremely hard material.

Zambel approached it, and looked along its length.

"It's difficult to see how far it reaches, but it continues in an almost perfectly straight line for hundreds of metres in each direction. It will not be difficult to climb."

Without further delay, they started to scale the cliff. For a Zargan, climbing vertical faces is not difficult, and the ascent took them only ten minutes. When they had clambered over the lip at the top, they were confronted with yet another obstacle. But this obstacle was so huge that both Zambel and Lam remained speechless for several seconds. In their amazement, they did not even bother to turn and look out over the tops of the trees behind them.

"We are now faced with another problem," reported Zambel, keeping calm. "On top of the cliff we have just climbed is another cliff. But it is not a cliff. It is *six kilometres high,* and *it is a building*." He paused to take in his breath. "It rises vertically in front of us, predominantly white in colour, but with some darker patches. One of the darker patches, which starts perhaps a kilometre above our heads, is perfectly rectangular. The blue sky is reflected from it, so I believe it is a window. It is this evidence that makes me believe this is a building: constructed by the intelligent life of this planet. As I speak, Lam is doing calculations."

"Yes," said Lam. "And the result is this: if the building is scaled down to the size of one of our buildings on Zarg, then the intelligent life on this planet is at least *two thousand times* bigger than we are."

"And that makes *us* the size of insects," Zambel concluded.

They gazed up at the unimaginably large building for several minutes. The base of it was only a hundred metres or so from where they stood on the edge of the small cliff, but they had to look almost vertically to see its top against the sky. Only when their necks and eyes ached from looking did they turn around and gaze out across the expanse of trees that now lay below them.

"We must begin to think of everything in terms of scale," said Zambel into his transmitter. "This is not a forest that we have climbed through, even though it stretches as far as we can see, thousands of kilometres to the horizon, across hills hundreds of kilometres high. To the creatures of this planet, it is grass."

Lam had been calculating again.

"If the intelligent beings who put up this building are at the top of the food chain, as is normal in our experience of planetary life-forms, then we must expect to find many voracious creatures – their insects – which will be a great danger to us."

Lam's words were almost like a signal. No sooner had he spoken than they observed, only fifty feet away, an enormous creature lumbering over the top of the first cliff. It was reddish-brown in colour, ten metres in length, and it had six legs and huge mandibles.

Lam and Zambel started to run, but soon realised that the creature – to them it was like an enormous horse – was extremely slow. They saw it placing each of its legs deliberately one in front of the other. It was swaying its head slowly from side to side as it watched them and picked up their scent. It started to lumber towards them.

In a one-to-one situation, the big slow-moving creature was no problem to the nimble Zargans. It was only as they turned that they saw the others. There were scores of them, climbing up the cliff at odd angles, most of them taking an interest in the two explorers. As soon as they realised that direct escape was impossible, Zambel and Lam took up positions with their backs against the vertical building and unstrapped their bolt-guns. They did not want to harm any creature on a host planet, but they had no choice if their own lives were threatened. As the first few six-legged 'horses' came inexorably towards them with their powerful mandibles open, they had no choice.

Lam fired the first bolt. Tipped with poison, it hit the first horse between the eyes. The horse went down with a crash. The other creatures paid no attention to the loss of their comrade, but continued towards them. Lam and Zambel fired bolt after bolt, and their attackers went down one after another. Still the creatures kept coming. They appeared as if from nowhere, wandering up and down in eccentric paths. Sometimes they walked away, but always their erratic progress brought them back in the Zargans' direction. Most of them came too close for the Zargans to leave their intentions to chance.

"We must work our way back to the capsule," said Zambel. "If we run out of bolts, we will be finished. I doubt if our speed through the jungle will be enough to save us if there are hundreds more in there."

"And that is where they are coming from," said Lam. He paused to fire another bolt, then said, "They must be the creatures that live in the huge caves we saw. We have landed on top of them!"

"And now that they have woken up," said Zambel, grimly,

"they are looking for their breakfast."

They gradually worked their way towards the cliff edge again, only firing when absolutely necessary. Lam stood at the cliff top while Zambel climbed down, then Zambel covered Lam's descent. In the trees their difficulties were less serious. They were able to hide until the creatures had passed by, then make further headway back to the capsule. When they were safely inside, they counted their remaining bolts and discovered that they had killed over two hundred of the creatures.

Through their diamond portholes, the Zargans watched the jungle outside. Red horses were everywhere now, climbing slowly up and down the blade-trees around the capsule. Gradually, the activity died down, and when no horse had been seen for half an hour, Zambel decided that it was safe to go out again.

"I shall go with Mogon this time," he said. "We will take five hundred bolts between us. Lam – you will stay here and monitor our progress. Whatever the odds, we must find some way of travelling the twelve thousand kilometres to the mother ship – even if we have to build a missile, and it takes us ten years to do it. But first we must learn about our natural enemies, and perhaps remove ourselves to a safer camp."

Zambel and Mogon made rapid progress through the jungle, and quickly scaled the low cliff. The ledge was clear in both directions for as far as they could see, which was several kilometres each way. Zambel chose to travel north, since their ship lay in that general direction. As they went, they steered round the bodies of red horses.

They had not gone far when, several kilometres in front of them, the edge of the artificial building suddenly appeared to bulge slowly outwards towards the sky. As they watched they realised that it was not the building itself that was moving, but something almost as massive that was moving round it.

It came very slowly, a huge, giant figure. Soon, they could make out an upper limb, then a head, then a lower limb. The whole creature began to fill the sky for several kilometres. As each limb was lifted slowly and replaced, the ground trembled, and the jungle beneath its mighty tread was crushed flat. The trees, unbroken, sprang slowly back into place as each limb was removed and placed again. As they continued to watch, fascinated by the experience of seeing real giants, two more began to appear, even larger than the first.

"They are coming towards the capsule!" Mogon shouted suddenly.

They were helpless to do anything, other than to warn Lam inside, as a great limb came inexorably down towards them. It avoided their ledge altogether, but came down only fifty metres from where the capsule lay. Lam reported that he could see it through his window.

"The foot is enormous – almost half a kilometre long, and a hundred and fifty metres wide. It seems to be encased in some artificial material."

"Like us, the giants are clothed," said Zambel, and then continued with some reverence: "I think, fellow Zargans, that we are looking at the intelligent life of this planet!"

The three giants then stayed perfectly still. Only a few seconds elapsed before Lam's voice came back over their headsets.

"The giant's foot has disturbed the red horses!" he shouted in alarm. "Watch out up there!"

"Thank you for the warning," said Zambel.

From their vantage point, they saw one of the creatures climbing on to the giant's foot. Before long, the foot was slowly raised. The Zargans detected sounds like the distant rumbling of thunder. Another long time passed, and they realised that the giants had turned their huge heads and eyes downwards in their direction.

"Take cover!" shouted Zambel.

Slowly, the massive bodies started to bend towards them. Three huge heads, each one almost half a kilometre in diameter, filled the sky above them. It was an awesome sight.

Zambel and Mogon had taken refuge behind one of the dead red horses. A long time passed again without any apparent move from the giants. Only the low rumbling continued.

Then Lam noticed that another horse had come over the lip of the cliff and was walking slowly in their direction. It paused on its journey to examine the body of one of its fellows, then continued to come directly towards them. Before it came too close, Lam fired a bolt. The creature collapsed and lay still.

Another long time passed. The giants went away, then later came back. When they returned, their massive hands slowly scooped up several of the horses' bodies and took them away. Then the giants were gone.

Zambel and Mogon decided to return to the capsule to allow the red horse activity to die down, and to discuss the situation with Lam.

"I only hope," said Zambel, "that we have not been shooting their sacred pets."

CHAPTER FIVE

The Brooch

After a hurried journey down Drift Hill, over the long straight road, and across the undulating valley floor, the three children arrived at Fell Farm. They were breathless and excited.

Helen and Jimmy's mother was there. She greeted them all with big smiles.

"So this is your new friend, is it?" she said.

Helen introduced her properly to Sam.

"Can we borrow Dad's microscope?" said Helen, wasting no time. Then, without waiting for an answer, "Where is it?"

"We want to look at some red ants," said Jimmy.

"Well, I hope they keep still," said Mrs Wallace. She laughed. "They'll walk off the slide if you're not careful."

"They're dead, silly," said Jimmy, sighing. "That's why we want to look at 'em."

"Where is it?" said Helen anxiously. "Where's the microscope?"

In Dad's study in the big cupboard – and mind you don't touch anything else—"

Her words trailed off as her two offspring stampeded towards the study like a herd of miniature elephants. Sam stood politely waiting for permission to stampede with them.

"You're staying with Mr Black, I hear?" said Mrs Wallace.

"Yes," said Sam. "Only for three weeks."

"That's a long way to send you – from London, isn't it?"

"Yes."

Mrs Wallace looked straight at him.

"Is Mr Black looking after you properly without his wife

there?" she said. She seemed concerned.

"I suppose so," said Sam.

"What do you mean, you suppose so? Either he's looking after you properly, or he isn't."

"Well, I haven't really been there long enough yet. That's what I mean."

"I can't understand him. He's in-and-out and in-and-out and in-and-out all day long, and he's often out half the night. I sometimes wonder what he gets up to. . . Does he feed you properly?"

The young elephants came charging back again and trampled on Sam's answer.

"Got it!" shouted Helen from two feet away. The herd galloped past and was gone.

"It's like living in a train tunnel!" Mrs Wallace laughed. She gave Sam a little push towards the running, shouting, excited throng of two that had disappeared through the door and up to Helen's bedroom.

Upstairs, Helen almost threw the polished wooden box on to her bed. As soon as Sam arrived, the three of them pressed in close to look at it.

The equipment inside the box was old, and some of the shiny coating had been rubbed away. Helen set up the brass stand and screwed the barrel to it. She took out a little assembly with a lens at each end – the eyepiece – and screwed it into the top of the barrel.

"The bottom end's more difficult," she said. She pointed to a little line of individual lenses. They ranged from fat to thin, and lay in their little velvet pouches on a shelf inside the box. "We can choose different magnifications, see? Let's try this one."

She selected one from the middle of the row, unscrewed another little assembly, dropped the lens carefully into it, then screwed it up again. Then she pushed the whole thing into the bottom end of the barrel.

"Now we need some light," she said.

"You look as if you've used this before," said Sam.

"Ponds are best," said Jimmy. "You get squiggly things in ponds."

Helen turned the microscope towards the window. She tilted the little mirror underneath until it reflected the light back up the barrel and into her eye.

"That's it," she said. "Now – where's an ant?"

Carefully, Sam took the old seed packet from his pocket. He shook one of the dead ants on to the glass slide that Helen held out for him. She pushed the slide into the little grips on the stand below the barrel, then turned the big knob to focus it. She moved the slide around, then said, "Look!"

Sam looked. Under the microscope, the ant looked huge. The light coming from the mirror underneath put it partly in silhouette, but there was more light coming directly from the window above. It was easy to see what had caused Helen's exclamation. Sticking out of the side of the ant's head, just near its eye, was something that resembled the top half of an arrow. It was perfectly straight, like a metal rod, and it had tiny "flights" at the end. It stuck out as far as a third of the width of the ant's head.

"It's an arrow!" said Sam. "I'm sure it's an arrow!"

By this time Jimmy was jumping up and down wanting his turn. Sam moved aside to let him see.

"What do you think?" Sam went on. "Shall we look at another one?"

Jimmy couldn't see what the fuss was about. Helen drew a picture for him to compare with the view in the microscope, and at last he could understand it.

She took another of the ants, and put that on the slide. The story was the same. This time, a thin, tufted rod stuck out a quarter of a millimetre in front of its head, between its eyes.

"Let's try and get one out!" said Sam.

"What – the arrow – or whatever it is?" said Helen.

49

"Of course! We'll see all of it, then. Has your mum got any tweezers – really fine tweezers?"

"I think so! I'll ask!"

Two minutes later, Helen was back with some tweezers – not as fine as Sam had hoped, but good enough to try.

"I'll need something like a needle to hold the ant still. . ."

"Jimmy – go and get a needle."

Jimmy obediently raced out and raced back with a pin.

"That'll do," said Helen.

The next ten minutes was spent with Sam and Helen taking it in turns, trying to grasp the tiny end of the whatever-it-was with the huge end of the tweezers. It was like trying to get someone's splinter out with a two-ton mechanical grab. They sent Jimmy for the thinnest needle their mother could find. At last, by a combination of teasing with the needle, and pulling with the tweezers, the object came out.

"It's just got an ordinary point," said Helen, who had been the one to succeed, "but the back end looks like an arrow, all right. Let's measure it."

She pushed a transparent plastic ruler under the microscope alongside the arrow, and lined it up with the millimetres.

"It's exactly half a millimetre long," she announced.

Then Jimmy had a look, then Sam.

"They've been killed with *bows and arrows*!" Sam said at last. "*The ants have been killed with bows and arrows!*"

"Or a crossbow," said Helen.

"Or whatever. . . But it means. . ." Sam started calculating. "If our arrows are half the length of a man… and these arrows are the same… *then whatever fired them is only… a millimetre tall!*"

For some moments they considered Sam's calculations in silence. Then Helen said, "Do you think it's anything to do with the UFO we saw?"

"I don't see how," said Sam. "It went right over the hill at the back."

"No…" Helen agreed. "It didn't look as if anything fell actually *in* your uncle's garden."

"Perhaps it hasn't landed at all. Perhaps it's parachuted thousands of little green men all over the countryside. Perhaps they're invading us!"

Helen looked horrified.

"We ought to tell someone."

"Tell someone what?" Mrs Wallace's voice came into the room behind a big tray of drinks and home-made cakes.

"We think a UFO has landed and dropped little tiny space people behind Mr Black's house. . ." said Helen.

"And they're killing all the ants!" put in Jimmy.

"Oh, well, *we've* got nothing to worry about then, have we?" said Mrs Wallace, and laughed.

"No, but you must see!" said Helen. She made her mother look at one of the ants through the microscope.

After a few moments Mrs Wallace stopped trying to look through the eyepiece and said, "Oh, it's no use. I can never see in those things. You'll have to show your father!"

"Well, that wasn't much use," said Helen, when her mother had gone.

"She probably thinks we're just playing a game," said Sam. "Like grown-ups usually do."

Sitting on the bed, they tucked into the refreshments that Mrs Wallace had brought them, discussing their immediate plans in between mouthfuls.

"I say we go and look for the aliens," said Helen. "We can start by looking round the ants' nest."

"They're too small," said Sam. "If they're intelligent – which they must be – they'll just hide from us."

"But we can still look. We might find *something*!"

Sam had every intention of looking.

"Yes," he agreed. "We might find *something*."

*

From the farm they could see Uncle Black's car outside Drift Hill Cottage. They decided to avoid the chance of being seen by Sam's uncle as much as possible. This meant a game in which they crawled on their stomachs most of the way up the fell. Twenty minutes later found them climbing over the fence to the east of Drift Hill Cottage. This way, they could approach the outbuilding from the rear without being seen from the house.

They squatted down near where they had found the ant's nest. Jimmy soon complained that he had been shot with an arrow already, and stayed at a respectful distance.

Carefully, they searched through the grass near the little heap of earth. It was Helen who spotted the thing first.

"Look!" she said. "I've found a diamond brooch!"

She held it up and watched it sparkle in the sun. It was cylindrical, about two centimetres long and one in diameter, mostly made of metal. Around its circumference, at regular intervals, they could see little diamonds.

"Funny looking brooch," said Sam. "Let me have a look." He took it and turned it over in his hands.

They were standing up now, and Helen suddenly saw something through the window of the outbuilding.

"Your uncle's coming!" she said, suddenly.

Sam swung round and looked. His Uncle Black, grim-faced and scruffy, was approaching fast, not heading for the door this time, but coming round the back.

"You two go!" said Sam.

Helen grabbed her brother and pushed him round the outbuilding the opposite way to Sam's uncle. Sam stood his ground and waited to see what his uncle wanted.

"I want to talk to you!" was his first comment as he rounded the corner and turned his glowering face on Sam.

Sam sensed that his uncle was in a foul mood about something. Instinctively, he started to back off. His uncle took two sudden leaps and caught him by the shirt collar.

"What have I done?" said Sam.

"You've been disobedient, that's what you've done! Not only no manners, but not to be trusted, either!"

He started to shake Sam violently back and forth.

"What do you mean?" said Sam.

"What do I mean?" said Uncle Black. He shook Sam even harder. "I thought I told you to stay in the kitchen and your bedroom!"

"I did!" said Sam. His ears were ringing and he was frightened.

"I see. Little liar now, as well, are we?" The shaking was redoubled. "Well, little liar – I know for a fact you've been snooping round the house while I was out. Thought you were clever, didn't you, little Mr Smart Sam Johnson?"

He then shook him so hard that it pulled Sam's shirt out of his jeans, and the creased letter from his aunt fluttered to the ground.

"What's that?" said Uncle Black, releasing Sam's collar and grabbing the letter. Sam tried to grab it at the same time, but instead, the brooch that Helen had found slipped from his hand. It rolled in the grass, glinting in the sunshine.

"And something else!" said Uncle Black, seizing it. "Let's have a look, shall we? Something you've stolen from the house, no doubt." He peered at it. "A diamond brooch, eh? That'll be worth a bob or two!"

"It's not mine!" said Sam. "You can't take it, it's not mine!"

"Whose is it, then?"

Sam didn't answer.

"So you stole it?"

Still no answer.

"In that case, I'll have it. That'll help to pay for your keep." He slipped the brooch in his pocket and started reading the letter.

As his uncle scanned the single sheet, Sam looked up at

him in horror, realising how stupid he'd been to hide the letter instead of destroying it.

His uncle only took three seconds to realise what it said, and looked furious. He suddenly made a grab for Sam's collar again and, dragging Sam beside him, circled back towards the house.

"So this is the letter you *didn't get*, is it?" he said ominously, his eyes glaring. "The letter you didn't get, telling you the holiday was off? Well now! Since you're not supposed to be here... *and since you knew all along you're not supposed to be here...*" he went on slowly, "it means you're not to be trusted. I won't feel bad about locking you in your room now. And you won't say anything to your parents about being locked in, and I won't say anything to them about this letter, see? What would your parents say if they knew you had this? You've only got yourself to blame. After three weeks in there you'll begin to wish you'd listened to your Uncle Jeremy in the first place and not gone snooping around."

They reached the top of the stairs.

"It also means you've lost the use of the kitchen, so it's cold food for you, matey! Give me that back door key!"

Sam fumbled in his pocket and found the key. His uncle took it and pushed Sam into his room. He slammed the door and locked it, and gave Sam his parting comment.

"Think yourself lucky you're getting any food at all!" he said.

Sam heard the heavy thud of feet on the thin stair carpet, then silence.

Sam was stunned. Events had moved so quickly that he'd hardly had time to catch his breath. It was only as he nursed his aching head that the full meaning of what had happened occurred to him.

How could his uncle have known that he had looked round

54

the house? Jimmy had warned them as soon as the yellow car had appeared over the hill, so his uncle couldn't have seen them inside the house. And they'd left everything exactly as they'd found it.

Even worse, he had stupidly kept the letter and was now confined to his room, totally powerless to do anything about it. Because of the letter, he wouldn't even be able to tell his parents.

Worst of all, he had even more stupidly let his uncle see the brooch they'd found. His uncle would probably sell it. Sam felt devastated. The shock of his uncle's reaction had been completely unexpected. Sam had been so anxious to grab the letter, he hadn't given the brooch a second thought.

It was a few years since Sam had felt like crying, but he came close to it now. His ears were singing, his head was throbbing, and his eyes felt heavy and prickly with tears.

But he didn't cry. Instead, he went to the window.

Helen and Jimmy were standing halfway down the hill, looking up at the cottage. Sam waved at them, but they probably couldn't see into the dark interior of the room. He didn't want his Uncle Black see his friends, so he didn't approach the window, and didn't try to open it.

Instead, another idea was slowly forming in his brain. He didn't want to spoil it now by letting his uncle see that Helen and Jimmy were involved.

That afternoon, Sam's uncle pushed some food and drink into Sam's room and then went off in his car.

After eating the unsatisfying meal, Sam went to his window and opened it without too much difficulty. He put his head out and found that there were no convenient drainpipes. It just wasn't possible to climb down. It was also too far to jump, even if he hung from the sill.

His door, too, was firmly locked. Probing the keyhole with a wire coat hanger produced no reason for hope.

Most of the afternoon he lay on his bed, thinking. Occasionally he stood up to see if Helen and Jimmy were anywhere to be seen, but they didn't appear. It seemed odd, because they could see that his uncle's car was gone, and easily come up.

Later in the afternoon, Sam heard the noise of a car approaching. It didn't sound as rattly as his uncle's car, so he put his head out of the window to look. It was one of those foreign cars with the big springs at the back. It skidded jerkily to a halt outside the cottage, and an elderly woman climbed out of the driving seat.

Sam realised with horror that it was the old lady from the train. What on earth was *she* doing here? It would be far too much of a coincidence for her to know Uncle Black. . . No – she knew where Sam was staying because she'd read the address on his luggage. She'd remarked on it, and Sam had told her lies about it, as well.

Sam was not sure whether he gasped, or made a noise, but for some reason the woman looked up and saw him.

"There you are, you naughty boy!" she said. She was wearing a smile, and Sam realised with a sinking heart that all had been forgiven. But what was she doing here?

"Hello," he said.

"Am I to crick my neck, or are you coming down to talk to me?"

"What about?"

"Come down and I'll tell you, little boy."

"I can't come down," said Sam. "I'm locked in."

"What do you mean, locked in? People don't get *locked in* these days!"

"I do," said Sam, with perfect truth for once.

"Nonsense! Let me see!"

"You can't get in. The back door's locked as well, and I can't get down to open it."

"I'll have to stand back," said the lady. "I'm getting neck-

ache." She took a few paces back. "That's better! Now.
Tell me why you are locked in. It must mean that your
'treatment' is not being as successful as your parents might
have hoped?"

"Treatment?" asked Sam, frowning.

"I *thought* you said you were here to curb your tendency to
tell lies, little boy. That's what you told me. But that was a
lie as well, of course. I have an *excellent* memory, you see.
You said that Mr Black is one of the country's leading
criminal psychologists, I believe?"

"Oh – yes." The train journey seemed ages ago, and Sam
had forgotten most of his lies already.

"What have you been doing while you've been here?"

"Why did you come?" said Sam, ignoring her question.
He couldn't contain his curiosity any longer. "You don't. . .
you don't *know* Mr Black, do you?"

"I came, little boy, because you left your book on the train!
That's why I came! I tried to find you on the station, but
you'd gone. But I remembered your address, and I
remembered your name and I remembered everything about
you. So what could be easier than to take a drive in the
country and deliver it myself! I live in Carlisle, you see."

"Yes," said Sam, "I remember. I-I mean – I mean, thank
you. I wondered what had happened to it."

The old lady propped herself against the wing of her car.

"Now you can tell me about your 'treatment'. What has
happened so far?"

"I've been locked in my room," said Sam. "You couldn't
get me out, could you?"

"But I'd be interfering with your *treatment*, dear boy. If
Mr Black is the *best criminal psychologist* in the country,
I'm *sure* he knows what he's doing."

Sam was snookered. Had he told his lies too well? Was
the old lady really that gullible? Sam didn't think so. It
sounded more likely that she was getting her own back.

"He's not *really* a criminal psychologist," he said.

The old lady smiled and wagged her finger at him.

"You can't fool me, you know!" she said. "You're *fibbing* again so that I'll be tempted to let you out!"

"I'm not fibbing, honestly," said Sam. "He's not a criminal psychologist." His quick eyes flitted back and forth, doing calculations. "I could easily jump on to the roof of your car if you moved it under here."

The old lady was horrified.

"You are not jumping on to the roof of my nice little car!"

"There might be a ladder round the back," suggested Sam.

"I don't care if there is a ladder," said the old lady. "I'm not letting you out. I think it's refreshing, after all, to think that there's some *discipline* left in the world. The modern generation has had it far too soft!"

Sam changed tack.

"I haven't had any food," he said.

The old lady smiled and wagged her finger again.

"It won't work!" she said. "I'm not letting you out! Perhaps it will teach you a lesson! You sneaked away from me on the train when I was asleep, and you thought you'd never see me again! You didn't realise what a good memory I have! And you were in such a hurry to get out, you stupidly left your book on the seat. I think you *deserve* to be locked up without any food!"

Sam groaned inwardly. He had run out of ideas.

"What's more," the old lady went on, "I have taken an interest in you. I shall come back in a few days time to see how you are progressing with your *untruthfulness*. Perhaps I might be able to meet the great *criminal psychologist* himself!"

Sam was speechless. The old lady stood up. She tossed his book up towards the window with a deft flick of her wrist. Sam caught it and thanked her.

"I used to be a netball captain!" she explained, proudly.

Then she climbed back into her car, crashed the gears, turned in a big circle on the bumpy grass verge, and headed back towards Carlisle.

Sam put his chin in his hands and watched the car bouncing out of sight. He suddenly realised that he was in an even bigger mess than he'd originally thought.

To console himself, he picked up *The Galaxy of Doom*. He was glad she had brought it back, but he hoped he had seen the last of her.

He turned to the page where he had left off, and started to read.

CHAPTER SIX

The Search

In between snacks and drinks, Sam read his book. Occasionally, he looked out of the window to check for any sign of Helen and Jimmy, but saw none. There was an estate car at the farm that hadn't been there earlier, but no sign of his friends.

His plan, as soon as it was dark, was to signal to the farmhouse with his torch. The only problem was that Sam didn't know much Morse code. He knew S-O-S (dot-dot-dot, dash-dash-dash, dot-dot-dot), but he was reluctant to use that in case someone else saw it and thought it was a real emergency. He knew the letter 'E' because that was a single dot, and he remembered 'T' because that was a single dash. He also knew 'A' (dot-dash) and 'M' (dash-dash) because he knew how to signal 'SAM'.

Putting down this complete vocabulary of S,O,E,T,A,M, Sam thought it looked like a bad draw at *Scrabble*. He tried to mix the letters into sensible words to make up a message. Most of his afternoon was spent doing anagrams, and he finally came up with "MEET SAM AT OME". He felt that it somehow lacked the dignity that a cry for help should have. He wished he could remember what 'H' was. Eventually, he decided on just "MEET SAM".

Uncle Black had not returned, and when it began to get dark, Sam abandoned his book and started to put his plan into action. He switched off his bedroom light. Standing well back from the window so that no one near the house would be able to see him, he started flashing his torch on and off. He pointed it at the farmhouse, knowing that Helen and

Jimmy were fond of looking out of their window at night.

Sam signalled for over half an hour. He saw an upstairs light go on in the farmhouse at ten o'clock, and a quarter of an hour later he saw it go off. Five minutes after that, he was relieved and excited to see the dot-dash-dash of a dim light answering his own.

Unfortunately, Sam couldn't read the message that was coming back. He wrote it down faithfully. He recognised the occasional 'E' and 'A' and a couple of the other letters he knew, but when the flashing stopped he couldn't make any sense of it at all. To Sam, it said:

.--,E,....,A,...-,E,-...,E,E,-.,O,..-,T,A,.-..,
.-..,-..,A,-.--,....,O,.--,A,.-.,E,-.--,O,..-

which wasn't really a lot of help.

Sam decided to send his complete vocabulary. He signalled "A,E,M,O,S,T" over and over again. This produced a repeat of the first message from the farmhouse, but Sam interrupted. This time he separated the letters he knew with a long, long flash for each missing letter. He was soon rewarded with a message twenty-six letters long. He recognised each of the letters he already knew in its right place in the alphabet.

"Good old Helen!" he said aloud, impressed. "She's given me the whole alphabet!"

He immediately tried it out by signalling "THANKS" and was rewarded with the reply "AT LAST". Then a conversation developed. Sam translated the first message Helen had sent, and it said, "WE HAVE BEEN OUT ALL DAY. HOW ARE YOU?"

Sam replied, "LOCKED IN MY ROOM."

"I WILL RESCUE YOU."

"WHEN BLACK ASLEEP. NOT DAYTIME."

"OK. NOW."

"NO. BLACK NOT BACK."

"OH. HAVE YOU LOOKED AT BROOCH THING."

"NO. BLACK HAS IT."

"DAMN. OOPS SORRY. LANGUAGE."

Sam laughed.

"WE GET IT TONIGHT. I WILL SAY WHEN BLACK IN AND ASLEEP. YOU BRING STRING, ROPE, PLASTICINE, SAFETY PINS, STIFF WIRE."

"OK."

There was a pause, and then Sam flashed back, "YOU ARE BRILLIANT."

"ME NOT BRILLIANT, IT IS MY TORCH."

"SILLY."

"YOU SAY I AM BRILLIANT, NOW YOU SAY I AM SILLY. MAKE UP YOUR MIND."

"BRILLIANT."

"I THOUGHT SO."

"SEE YOU LATER."

"OK."

It was past midnight when Uncle Black returned in his car. Sam heard him come in, and heard him come straight up the stairs and into his room. Looking out of his own window, Sam could see the yellow patch of light that strayed out of his uncle's window. Before long it disappeared as his uncle went to bed.

"Good," thought Sam. "He's probably had too much to drink."

Within minutes there was the sound of heavy snoring. Sam took up his torch and flashed "ALL CLEAR."

The answer came back, not from the farmhouse, but from halfway up the hill. "I AM HERE."

Once again, Sam could not help admiring Helen's initiative. She had obviously spent the time collecting together all the things they needed. Then she had made her way towards the cottage to be ready for when his signal came. It was probably the best way for her to stay awake, as well, he thought.

Soon, Helen was standing under his window, whispering.

"Hello."

"Hello."

"I've tried the ladder, but it's too heavy for me to move it without making a noise," she said.

"Climbing up here with rope won't be easy," whispered Sam. "But if I come down on the rope I can help you get the ladder."

"Okay."

Helen coiled the rope and threw it. Sam caught it on the third throw. He tied the end to one of the feet of his bed. Then, hoping that his weight wouldn't lift the bed and make a noise, he tested it, then eased himself on to the sill. He soon discovered that climbing down was not as easy as he had thought. It seemed to Sam that he was making a lot of noise, and being very awkward. But before long he was on the ground next to Helen. They were both excited at their success.

Then they went to get the ladder, an old one with wooden rungs. Soon, they were both back in Sam's room, relieved to hear the loud snoring from next door. But they still spoke in whispers.

"We've got to pick my lock with a bent safety pin, or some wire," said Sam. "Did you manage to get any?"

Helen produced a bag with everything Sam had asked for.

"I couldn't get plasticine," she apologised, "but I found some putty. I bet it was for making an impression of the key!"

Sam smiled in delight.

"You bet!" he said. "If it works, I'll have the run of the whole house any time I want!"

"Who's going to make it?"

"We can! There are some old tools in the shed outside. We can have a go, anyway."

"This is exciting!" said Helen. "Poor little Jimmy's fast

asleep, but he couldn't possibly have come up for this sort of thing. He helped me do the signalling, though. I made him go and get the encyclopaedia with the Morse code in as soon as we saw the flashing."

"So you didn't know it, either!"

"No. It was a good job we knew what you meant in the end. We couldn't think what on earth 'AEMOST' meant until you started spacing it out."

"Let's have a go at this door, shall we?"

Getting out of Sam's room proved much easier than they expected. Uncle Black had left the key in the door, but hadn't turned it round to stop it being pushed out. It meant that Helen and Sam could use the oldest trick in the world.

The only large piece of paper they could find was a sheet lining Sam's suitcase. They slid it under the door, pushed out the key with a safety pin, and dragged the paper back into the room with the key on it. The whole operation took only a few minutes, and Uncle Black's snoring still rattled on.

"He sounds like a pig with indigestion," said Helen.

"He is a pig," said Sam. "And I hope he's got indigestion from drinking too much."

The next thing they did was to make firm impressions of the key in the soft putty that Helen had brought. Helen did a drawing of the key as well, to make sure that it could be copied accurately. Then, with torches in hand, they unlocked the door and tiptoed into Uncle Black's room.

He was lying on the top of his bed with most of his clothes on. He had managed to take off his shoes and his jacket, but that was all. The jacket was the same one that he had been wearing when he had taken the letter and the brooch off Sam. Sam felt in the pockets. He didn't find the letter, but the brooch was there, and also a large bunch of keys. He took them out and smiled at Helen in the torchlight.

They went back to Sam's room straight away. Sam locked

the door from the inside, and carefully put the brooch on top of the chest of drawers.

"He can't surprise us, now!" said Sam. "I don't know which of these keys we need, though."

"You're not going to keep them all?"

"No. But we can take impressions, can't we?"

Half an hour later, they had taken drawings and impressions of every key on the ring. To their delight, they found that there was a duplicate back door key on the ring. They took it off and kept it.

"You know what I want to do next?" said Sam.

"What?"

"Look in that room downstairs."

They were both feeling very tired by this time, but realised they might not have the opportunity again. Once more they unlocked Sam's door. They crept silently down the stairs and stood outside the mystery door. Sam tried turning the handle to see if it would open without a key, but it was locked. Quietly, he tried several keys from the key-ring. The third one unlocked the door, and they tiptoed in.

What they saw in the room was the last thing they could ever have expected. There were boxes and tins of food everywhere, heaps of clothes, newspapers and books. But in one corner, sprawled in a sleeping posture across a settee, was a man. He had short cropped hair, and was showing a few days' growth of a beard. Luckily for them, he was in a deep sleep.

Sam and Helen looked at each other open-mouthed in the torchlight. Sam nodded towards the door. They made a silent but hasty exit and went back upstairs. Sam replaced Uncle Black's keys, then they went to Sam's room and locked the door again.

"Well!" whispered Sam. "What do you think of that?"

"What on earth is *he* doing there?"

"I don't know," said Sam, thinking. "But it explains one thing. It explains how Uncle Black knew we were prowling around the house when he was out!"

"Yes, of course!"

"And it means that we can't do *anything* during the day! I can't even get out if I know Uncle Black's going to be gone all day, because that man will tell him!"

Now Helen was thinking.

"He can't be a prisoner," she said at last.

"Why ever not?"

"Because if he was a prisoner, he wouldn't have told your uncle we were prowling round. He would have attracted *our* attention and asked us to let him out!"

"You are brilliant, aren't you?" said Sam. "That means he's being *hidden*!"

"What from?"

"Only one thing. The police."

"Do you think he's an escaped convict? He looked like it with that hair of his."

Sam clapped his hands together silently.

"So *that's* why Uncle Black didn't want me here!" he said.

"The man's hiding until the heat wears off, or whatever you call it," said Helen.

Sam was quiet for a minute or two. Then he suddenly jumped up.

"I'm going to look at those newspapers!" he said.

"Sam! You can't! It's too risky to go down there a second time!"

"But if he's escaped recently, they'll say so. The room's full of them."

Helen was hesitant, as much from the onset of tiredness as from her natural fear of being caught.

"All right," said Sam. He realised it was her tiredness talking. "You go back, and we'll look at them tomorrow night."

"All right."

"Let's think. You take the back door key. Then you can get in tomorrow night and unlock my room. Can I keep the brooch? I want to try something out."

"I'm too tired to think of anything, so I don't care."

"Can you bring your father's microscope tomorrow night?" Helen yawned. "I'll try."

"Come on. We'll get you home."

Helen picked up her bag of useful implements, and they went quietly down the stairs together. The ladder was put back where it came from, then Helen came upstairs again. She locked Sam into his room and left the key in the door as it was before. She let herself out of the back door and locked it with the key they had taken.

Sam hauled in the rope and hid it in the bottom of his hold-all bag. He heard a whispered 'good night' coming through the open window, and popped his head out to say the same.

"Signal me when you're back," he whispered.

He watched the light from Helen's torch until it had reached the farm, then waited for her signal. It came five minutes later, a simple 'OK.'

Sam signalled 'OK' back, then closed his window and drew the curtains. He was feeling tired now, but his mind and his rapidly closing eyes were drawn like magnets to the top of the chest of drawers. The little diamond-studded object sat there, silent and mysterious. Sam didn't believe for one moment that it was a brooch. He remembered the UFO that had streaked out of the sky the night before, and his tired mind connected it with *The Galaxy of Doom*. In his wild imagination, the little object wasn't a brooch, it was a spaceship.

He undressed and climbed into bed. He looked at the little object with his torch for a while. What if his uncle came in in the morning before he was awake, and saw it? And what was he, Sam, going to do with it, anyway? He wanted to find out what it really was. It didn't look as if it could be opened without smashing it, and he didn't want to do that.

He reached inside his holdall and took out his travelling alarm clock and a small piece of paper. He propped the clock on the little legs that unfolded inside its case. He carefully placed the brooch inside, out of the way of any casual glance his uncle might give. He wrote on the piece of paper in block capitals, in the smallest writing he could manage, "WHO ARE YOU?", then carefully tore off the piece with the words on. It measured only one centimetre by a half. He put it inside the clock stand as well, facing the little diamonds that sparkled even in his torchlight.

He smiled to himself, switched off his torch, and was soon fast asleep.

He dreamed about trying to get the ladder on to the train, and finding his Uncle Black snoring inside it when he got home. He was still dreaming several hours later, when a tiny pencil of light sparkled from one of the diamonds, and scanned his piece of paper.

CHAPTER SEVEN

The Message

After their encounter with the giants of the planet, Zambel, Mogon and Lam sat in their capsule and attempted to analyse their situation.

"Things are not good," began Zambel. "If our capsule was repairable, we could fly back to the mother ship. But it is not, and we cannot. I am afraid we have little hope of getting back to the spaceship across twelve thousand kilometres of this terrain."

"We may just be unlucky," said Lam. "Outside this immediate area, we may find the planet's wildlife more hospitable."

"I think it unlikely," said Zambel. "But whatever happens, we must not give up. For all we know, ours may be the only Zargan Ark left in existence. If we cannot find a new home for our people, then our people will perish."

"We always have the ultimate option," said Mogon.

Zambel stared at him.

"You mean to open the Ark here and now, and release Zargankind on to this planet? It goes against the rules that have been laid down for the last five thousand years."

"But nevertheless, those rules state that, *in the last resort*, we can occupy a planet that already has intelligent life."

"But we know why the rule was made. If we are forced to occupy such a planet, the chances for our race to survive on it will be severely limited. Only one species can dominate a planet. Here, I'm afraid, that species seems to be two thousand times our size. It would not take many guesses to work out which of the intelligent species would survive in the end?"

"But we are so small, they cannot even see us."

"We cannot see the microbes that invade *our* bodies, but that does not mean that we cannot eradicate them."

"But the microbes that invade our bodies are not intelligent, Zambel. We are. Who is to say that with guile and invention we could not take over this planet?"

"Perhaps you would like to tell us, Mogon?" put in Lam. "How would *you* go about killing a giant that is three kilometres high, and is *eight billion times* as massive as we are?"

"We would have to think like the microbe," said Mogon. "We would first have to know our enemy, find out how he works, what his weaknesses are. We would then interfere with his food chain, or his chromosomes. Or perhaps introduce a poison into his environment that would wipe them all out within a matter of hours."

"It is not the way it should be," said Zambel. "They have as much right in this galaxy as we have. We are the homeless, not they. For them it is not necessary – yet. We have no right to take that away from them. We are not Gods."

Mogon sighed.

"Then you must tell us, Zambel, what are *your* plans for reaching the Ark?"

"With no command module, the sealed biosphere of the mother ship will survive for another fifty years. As you know, it is only the fifty-year maintenance that is required to keep the unit otherwise self-perpetuating."

"And if we three – we three who are entirely responsible for that maintenance – if we are wiped out tomorrow, the unit will last for fifty years, then gradually die?"

"You are forgetting your training, Mogon. It is possible for us to program an auto-release for, say, ten years' time, to unseal the unit and release our future generations on to the planet."

"Should we not have programmed that already?" said Mogon. "We are here discussing things that should have been done the moment we landed."

"Then why did you not suggest them?" said Zambel. He looked at Mogon with some distaste. "We are here to have a discussion, not an argument. If the discussion decides that is what we must do, then so be it."

"But you are the captain. You should have taken that step already."

"I think," said Lam, who had remained rather quiet, "that the shock of our experience here is beginning to fray our nerves. Let us program the ship now, then return to our discussions. At least we will be confident then, that if we perish in the meantime, the future of our race will be assured, at least for a while longer, on this planet."

"But I'm afraid it's not as simple as that," said Zambel. "I do not think that such programming will guarantee anything. Mogon is forgetting just how big the mother ship is. Its diameter is three hundred metres. Remember this – a giant of the planet was able to see *and pick up* one of the red horses that we killed – *within minutes of our killing it*. I do not think it will be long before beings with such fine senses find the mother ship. To them it will be perhaps seventy centimetres long, and fifteen centimetres wide."

Mogon was silent for a short while.

"So," Zambel went on, "we have to make a more difficult choice. It may be better to set the release program to function day by day. So that in the *absence of a signal* from us, the cargo will be released at the end of that day."

"That seems reasonable," said Lam.

"And in the meantime," continued Zambel, "we shall do everything in our power to reach the ship – however long it takes. We do not want to waste five thousand years for the sake of rushing now."

"Yes," said Mogon. "Yes. You are right. If there is one thing our race should have learned, it is patience." He looked up at Zambel. "I apologise for my remarks. We have had a good discussion, and we have reached a good decision."

"Let us send the program signal now," said Zambel.

"We estimate," said Zambel into the mission black box, "that the day on this planet is approximately twenty times as long as that on Zarg."

A long time had passed since their rather heated discussion. But now the programming had been set, and they were preparing to discuss their next moves.

"We have also noticed another curious phenomenon: the relationship between our perception of time, and that of the creatures of this planet. It seems that the larger the creatures, the slower they are. Creatures that are only a few times larger than us, such as the red six-legged horse, move around very sluggishly. It is only their large numbers that pose a threat to us.

"As for the giants, they move at a rate that is almost imperceptible at times. Whereas our footsteps are half a second apart when walking, those of the giants are as much as ten seconds apart. This also gives us the curious analogy that their perception of time, like the length of their day, is twenty times slower than ours. This may be caused by the enormous distances that their nerve messages have to travel. However, we cannot relax. Their limbs have also been observed to move at speeds of up to three kilometres per second!"

It was during these observations that the Zargans underwent their next experience. No one had been keeping watch through the portholes. Quite suddenly there was a tremendous jolt, not unlike that of rocket propulsion. When the capsule stabilised at last, they moved to the portholes and looked out. To their amazement their capsule was being held by one of the giants.

"They have found us!" shouted Mogon.

"That cannot be helped," said Lam. "Look at the view!"

For the first time the Zargans were able to see, from a reasonable height, the planet they had landed on. They could see the undulating green hills, and the huge structures that had been built by the giants.

For what seemed a long time, their capsule was accelerated and slowed in every direction as it was handled by the giants. They had their first view of the giants' faces, three hundred metres across, with eyes fifty metres in diameter.

And suddenly everything went dark.

The time that followed seemed endless to the helpless Zargans, battered by dizzying movements in an eternity of darkness. Shining lasers from within the capsule revealed nothing outside other than strange shapes and textures.

"Travelling through space is far better, with its view of the stars," Lam remarked, "than this sickening motion."

When at last their ordeal of darkness ended, they saw first some dim lights in the distance, then a much brighter, but still yellow, light all around them. They appeared to be inside a building now. Again their capsule was lifted and put down. Then it was placed within what could only be described as a metal superstructure. It was golden-yellow in colour, with great metal pieces protruding that appeared to have some symmetry of design. Eventually they observed a large white sheet inserted near them, only thirty metres from their windows. It was about half the size of their capsule, and it had hieroglyphics on it – strange shapes that meant nothing to the Zargans. And before they had time to observe it for long, the world outside was again plunged in darkness.

Zambel suggested that they all take a long rest. It was night on the planet once more, and further activity would be useless until the new day had begun.

They slept fitfully, although Zambel himself did not sleep much at all. Instead, he started grappling with their seemingly impossible problem. It was only much later that he started to think about the hieroglyphics. It occurred to him suddenly that they might be an attempt at communication.

While the others slept, Zambel switched on a laser torch. Carefully and steadily, he shone it out through the diamond window. Slowly and methodically, he began to copy the shapes that he saw on to a bio-screen.

At the same time, he wondered how he could respond. How was it possible to communicate with something that was eight billion times as massive? How could he talk to something that shared with him not the slightest fraction of understanding?

CHAPTER EIGHT

The Disaster

Sam woke up to the sound of his uncle opening the door and pushing food into the room. He looked at his watch. It was past ten o'clock.

"Still in bed, you lazy little so-and-so?" said Uncle Black.

Sam said nothing. Speaking out of place would only earn him more criticism. If he voiced some of his other thoughts, it would put his uncle on his guard. Sam only had one advantage left – surprise. The last thing he wanted was for his uncle to think he was planning something.

When his uncle had departed and locked the door again, Sam examined the tray from a distance. He was pleased to see a hot cup of tea and buttered toast and cereal. Sam felt almost grateful, half wishing he hadn't disobeyed orders and gone 'prowling around the house' after all. Midnight adventures were great, but the thought of midnight adventures for three weeks running didn't seem quite so much fun.

When Sam thought about the message he had written, propped up next to an old brooch, he felt silly and almost embarrassed. He had been tired and it had been late, and it had seemed a sensible thing to do at the time.

But space creatures only existed in stories. The ants had probably been killed by the shooting spikes of some plant or other, like nettles. The spikes on nettles had poison on the ends, and they would kill an ant straight away, Sam thought. It was probably a plant that had stung Jimmy in the first place, and not an ant at all.

He climbed out of bed and collected his breakfast tray.

Then he started wondering about the strange man they had seen during the night. He dearly wanted to know why he was there, and why he was keeping himself so quiet and out of sight.

He climbed back into bed with the tray on his lap. When he had finished eating he carefully put his travelling clock on the tray in front of him and peered into the inside of its little supports. The brooch was still there. He took out the piece of paper and looked at it. It still said "WHO ARE YOU?" just as he had written it the night before. Somehow, by some magic process, Sam expected it to have changed.

It was only when he was about to throw the paper back down again that he noticed the tiny marks underneath his message. He brought it back close to his eyes again, and nearly fell out of bed with shock when he saw what it was. Written in writing so tiny he could hardly read it, and right next to the bottom edge of the paper, was a repetition of his own message. It was set out exactly as he had written the original "WHO ARE YOU?".

Sam stared at the brooch in amazement. He screwed up his eyes to look at the paper again. The tiny writing really was there.

"Good grief!" he said aloud. Then, to himself, "There's something inside the brooch! There really is!"

It seemed funny to Sam that tiny alien creatures should ask who *he* was. He had only done it for fun, anyway, and he realised they couldn't possibly know what the message really meant. Whoever was inside had simply copied *his* message; what else could they do? By doing that, they were at least proving to him that they were intelligent, too.

Sam scrambled out of bed and dressed as quickly as he could. He put the breakfast tray by the door and tidied the room. He carefully removed the spaceship from under the clock. From now on it would always be a spaceship to Sam. He set it in the middle of the flat surface of the chest of drawers. He drew up the little chair and sat down. He took some paper and a fine pen from his bag, and thought for a moment. Then he drew, as small as he could, a picture of himself. When he had finished, he printed his name in tiny writing next to it. It looked something like this:

He propped it in front of the spaceship.

Then he waited.

When nothing had happened after ten minutes, Sam started to think all over again that he was being silly, or that he was still dreaming. He went to the window to see if he could see any sign of Helen or Jimmy, but there was none. Then he came back and sat watching the spaceship for another ten minutes. Still nothing happened.

Once again, Sam only really noticed the reply by accident: a tiny mark at the bottom edge of the paper that caught his eye. He strained forward to see what it was. It was a picture. Not a copied picture of Sam, but a different picture – and it was so small that Sam had difficulty seeing what it was really like. It seemed to have three arms sticking straight out of its top, and three legs underneath like a camera tripod. The total height of the drawing was only just over a millimetre, and Sam began to wonder if he was imagining that as well.

He went to the window again.

"I must be going mad," he said to himself. "See? I'm talking to myself now! And trying to converse with invisible creatures from outer space! If only Helen was here with the microscope. . . Then I'd know if I was seeing things or not!"

He watched as a car pulled away from the farmhouse across the valley. It snaked its way slowly to his right to join the middle of the long straight road, then turned back towards the village. As it swept along the straight, two little arms waved frantically from its windows. It was Helen and Jimmy, probably with their parents. Sam waved from behind his closed window and wondered where they were going. He hoped they wouldn't be gone all day.

After a lot of thought, he decided to draw some more pictures. He drew one to show the position of the Earth in our solar system, with himself standing on the Earth. It looked like this:

"I expect," said Sam aloud again, "that you already know where the Earth is in the solar system, because you've just landed on it. But this is to show you that *I* know where it is, as well."

On the same sheet of paper, he drew an ant with one of the arrows sticking into it, and next to it he copied as best he could the little three-legged, three-armed creature that they had drawn.

After that, still tired from his night's adventures, Sam lay on his bed and went to sleep.

He woke up to disaster. It was the sound of someone in

78

the room. When he opened his eyes, he saw that it was Uncle Black.

"How did you get this?" his voice was demanding. "It was in my pocket yesterday, and now you've got it back again. Where did you get it from?"

Sam, not fully recovered from his sleep, blinked at what his uncle was holding. It was the spaceship. He bolted upright and tried to snatch it back, but his uncle moved the hand away, holding Sam back with the other.

"How did you get it?" Uncle Black repeated.

"It's mine! You took it off me!"

"That's not what I asked. I took it off you yesterday. Now it's missing from my pocket, and you've got it back. How did you get it?" He made a threatening gesture.

Sam realised that open fighting was useless. He summoned up his inventive powers instead.

"You dropped it," he said. "When you – when you brought in the breakfast tray this morning. "I – I found it on the floor by the tray."

Uncle Black looked down at him for a few more moments, then turned away.

"Right. I'll put it somewhere without a hole in it this time," he said. He dropped it into the breast pocket of his shirt.

Sam stared from his uncle to the pocket in horror and dismay.

"But it's mine!" he said. His voice came out broken, and he felt his throat tighten up and his eyes starting to smart. "You can't take it!"

Uncle Black glared at him as he picked up the tray.

"Oh, yes, I can," he said. Then he dismissed the incident. "I'll be out most of the afternoon. I've brought you some more food. If you behave yourself, I might give you the run of the house again – but not for a couple more days. I don't want you prowling around, see?"

Sam had recovered himself, and saw very well. He knew exactly why his uncle didn't want him prowling around, and it made him even more determined to do something about it.

His uncle went out and closed the door, and Sam heard the key turn in the lock.

He sat on his bed and started to think. He was furious with himself for leaving the spaceship in full view and allowing himself to go to sleep. It was bad enough letting his uncle get hold of the spaceship the first time – although it hadn't seemed important then. But to let him take it *again* after all the trouble and danger he and Helen had gone through to steal it back – that was unforgivable. He felt ashamed and angry with himself, and he didn't know how he was going to break the news to Helen. She would think he was a complete idiot.

"I've got an IQ of minus five!" he said to himself, as his eyes wandered to the top of the chest of drawers where the spaceship had been. "I don't suppose my brain's any bigger than theirs..." Then he caught sight of his little piece of paper and, in a sudden movement, reached across and grabbed it.

His own pictures were there, just as he had left them. But all along the bottom of the little sheet were tiny, tiny marks. Just like before, Sam screwed up his eyes and tried to make them out. But they were too small to make any sense. They looked like pictures, not words, and they were impossible to decipher without a magnifying glass – or a microscope.

Very carefully, he put the paper inside his clock, and closed it up. He was so excited and so anxious to investigate the drawings on the paper that he went to the door and tried the handle, just to see if it was really locked. It was. He paced up and down the floor, turning every few steps because it was such a small room, thinking hard of what he could do. He wanted to look at the drawings. He wanted to know the identity of the man in the room downstairs. He wanted to know why he was keeping so quiet. But more than anything, he wanted to get the spaceship back. He *had* to.

Suddenly, he smiled to himself.

"It'll serve him right if it tries to take off in his pocket and burns a hole in his chest!" he said.

Shortly afterwards, Sam heard the sound of his uncle's car starting and moving off down the hill. He opened the window and watched it go. By the time it had disappeared from view, he had made up his mind on his next plan of action. It would be daring and dangerous, but with Helen's help, he could manage it.

CHAPTER NINE

The Escape

While Sam had been asleep, Helen's parents' car had returned to the farmhouse. Sam started to worry that Helen might venture towards the cottage during the day, forgetting the danger of being seen by the man downstairs. As the afternoon wore into evening, Sam was pleased to realise that Helen had had the sense to stay at home.

But as soon as it was dark, Sam started watching the farmhouse for clues to any activity within. He assumed that Helen and Jimmy had been sent to bed long before, but now he wanted to make sure their parents were asleep before he started signalling. It would cause a lot of problems if the adults happened to glance out of their window and read his messages.

At about eleven o'clock an upstairs light went on in the farmhouse. Ten minutes later it was extinguished. Sam gave it ten more minutes after that, then began signalling "HELLO" with his torch over and over again. Soon, an answer came back.

"HELLO. IS BLACK IN."

"NO."

"WHEN."

"HOPE SOON."

"STILL LOCKED IN."

"YES."

"GOOD NEWS."

"WHAT."

"CANNOT SAY OVER THE MORSE."

"HA HA."

"WELL YOU SAY SOMETHING FUNNY THEN."

"WISH BLACK WOULD COME."

"THAT'S NOT FUNNY."

"YOU ARE TELLING ME."

As the time slipped by, the torch conversation became more and more inane. Sam eventually called a halt when he realised he was in danger of running his batteries down. He needed to save enough to give an all-clear signal once Uncle Black was home, and snoring.

They didn't have much longer to wait. At about half-past eleven, the old Ford came rasping up the hill. For some unaccountable reason, Sam suddenly thought that he ought to get into bed. He didn't know why at first. Then he suddenly realised that if his uncle decided to look into his room, he would find him fully dressed, with a torch, at the window, and be suspicious straight away.

Sam quickly signalled "HUSH" with his torch, hoping that Helen would understand. Then he took off his outer clothes and shoes and slipped under the blankets. His heart was thumping as he heard his uncle climbing the stairs. Then – horrors! – he heard the key being quietly turned in his own lock. There was hardly a sound as the light went on. He sensed his uncle creeping towards the bed. Sam feigned a deep sleep.

"Are you awake?" his uncle's husky voice whispered. Then again, slightly louder: "Are you awake?"

Sam did not respond but tried to breathe evenly and lightly in spite of his pounding pulse. Then he heard his uncle murmur, "Good." The light went out, the door closed, and the key turned again.

Sam privately thanked whatever it was that had made him get into bed. He never wanted to be closer to discovery than that.

Presently, he heard the rumble of muffled voices downstairs – obviously his uncle with the man in the curtained room. They had wanted to make sure Sam was fast asleep before they started talking.

Sam dressed again, quietly, and went to the window.

"NOT CLEAR YET," he signalled, and received a brief "OK" in response.

Later, much later, his uncle mounted the stairs and went into his room. For a short while Sam also heard the man downstairs moving about. Then lights went out and he heard the snoring from his uncle's room. He waited another ten minutes, hoping that the man downstairs had also gone to sleep. He took up his torch and started the real business of the night.

"ALL CLEAR I HOPE," he signalled.

This time the reply was from the middle of the valley, near the straight road. It wasn't too long before Helen had let herself into the back door, unlocked Sam's door, and was sitting next to him on the bed, leaning against the wall.

"I'm so tired!" whispered Helen. "I don't think I can do this another night!"

"I don't think you'll have to," Sam whispered back.

Helen immediately woke up a little bit as Sam told her everything that had happened. He told her about the tiny writing of "WHO ARE YOU?" on the paper. He showed it to her, along with the drawing of the strange creature with three arms and three legs. Then he opened his clock and showed her the piece of paper with the tiny drawings along the bottom.

"I can't see what they are!" said Helen.

"I know. It's annoying. What we need is to look through that microscope of your father's. Did you manage to bring it?"

"I didn't dare. But what if I take this paper and the little brooch – I mean, the spaceship – and look at them at home tomorrow?"

"I don't think that's quite possible," said Sam, guiltily.

Helen looked at him sideways.

"Why not?"

Sam took a deep breath, let it escape in a long sigh, then told her the shameful news of how he had lost the spaceship again.

"Oh, *Sam!* You didn't!"

Sam looked suitably ashamed of himself while Helen told him what she thought of him. It was more or less a repeat of what Sam thought of himself.

"I know I'm stupid," Sam apologised, "but I was just so tired. I didn't think. And then I fell asleep."

"But now that we *know* there's something in there, we'll *have* to get it back again! And it mightn't be so easy this time."

"I'm really sorry, Helen, but at least I've decided what to do. The first thing is this: we don't tell any grown-up what we've really found. For one thing, they won't believe us. They'll think we're making up stories. None of them believe that things really might come from outer space. And if they really *did* believe in what we've found, *they'd want to interfere and spoil it*. They'd probably take it away from us altogether. They might even destroy it."

"Why would they do that?"

"That's what some grown-ups are like," said Sam. "In most of the space stories I've read, the grown-ups are always suspicious of everything. They think everything's a threat. And if whatever-it-is comes from outer space, they're even more suspicious. Because they don't understand it, they think it might harm the world."

"Well, it might," said Helen. "We didn't think of that."

"I did, a bit. But I think if they wanted to harm us, they'd've done it by now. They wouldn't be drawing pictures for us if they could just destroy us if they wanted to."

"Perhaps they're trying to find out if *we're* harmful?"

"Maybe. But they've landed here for a reason. It might be that they're just exploring, the same way we do. Or perhaps they were forced to land because of a problem. Or perhaps they really want to take over the planet."

"Or perhaps they're lost."

"I don't think they'd *land* if they were lost. It would be much easier to carry on in space without using any energy than to go to all the bother of landing." Sam grinned. "It's not like driving a car, where you pull on to the verge to look at your map!"

"So what do you think?"

"I think they've landed either to explore, or for supplies – but who knows? Could be anything."

Suddenly he noticed that Helen was grinning at him like a chimpanzee again.

"What are you laughing at?" he said.

"I've got some news."

"Really?"

Helen held out her palm and showed Sam five glittering new keys. Sam's mouth dropped open in surprise.

"How did you manage to get those?" he said, still keeping his voice to a whisper.

"We went into the village today – we waved at you from the car. Well – our cousin's the blacksmith. I made him swear on the bible that he wouldn't tell anyone. He cut the keys for me, but I had to promise that I wasn't doing anything *really* bad!"

"Helen, you're a genius!"

Helen looked pleased.

"So what's this plan of yours, then?" she said.

"Locked up in here, I can't do anything, that's the problem. And we can't keep waiting until lights-out to do the slightest thing. A few more nights without sleep and we'll be completely worn out."

"So?"

"So – I'm going to disappear!"

Helen's face lit up.

"You're *what?*"

"I'm going to disappear. I'm going to leave nasty Uncle Black with a mystery on his hands! That'll teach him a lesson!"

Helen quietly clapped her hands together in excitement.

"Sam! It sounds wonderful! Where are you going to disappear to?"

"That's where I need your help," said Sam. "And this is how I think we can do it. . ."

Apart from the sound of Uncle Black's snoring, the little cottage was silent as the two children crept out of Sam's room with his luggage. They carefully locked Sam's door, leaving the key exactly where Helen had found it, and tiptoed downstairs and out of the back door. They took great care to close that quietly, too.

The air was cool and fresh as they stepped outside. The lightest little breeze was blowing across the dark humps of the hills that straddled the horizon all around them. The stars were splashed across the dark sky as if God had been shaking a silver paintbrush.

Slowly and carefully, they made their way down to the farmhouse. They slipped into one of the outbuildings, and Helen showed Sam the place she had chosen. It was in the straw at the top of a steep wooden ladder.

"No one'll find you here!" she said. "We hardly ever use it at all, so no one's likely to come looking!"

The hay loft was deep and dark. It went back so far that Sam couldn't be seen from the ground, even by a six-footer standing against the far wall inside the building.

"It's perfect!" Sam pronounced. "Come on, let's dump the things and get back!"

"Are you sure about the next part?" said Helen. She

seemed anxious.

"Positive," said Sam.

"Come on, then."

Again they went out into the clear air. Again they crossed the rough grass of the valley, and climbed the long slope to the cottage. Helen opened the back door, then put the key back into her pocket. Together they quietly mounted the stairs. Uncle Black still snored. They let themselves into his room, then they began their search.

They found the shirt that Uncle Black had been wearing thrown on to a chair, but the spaceship wasn't in the breast pocket any more. They exchanged looks of bewilderment in the torchlight. Then they searched through all his clothing, and through all the places they could think of in his room. They were careful to put everything back as they had found it. But they didn't find the spaceship.

Sam made a gesture of looking at his watch, and nodded towards the farmhouse. Helen nodded back.

Sam accompanied Helen outside, where they were able to speak in whispers.

"Blast!" said Sam. "I wonder where he's hidden it?"

"It's horrible. We may never see it again."

"It's all my stupid fault. But we'll get it again, you'll see!"

"Are you *really* sure about the next bit?" asked Helen, still worried.

Sam nodded.

"They can't kill me. And if they catch me, they can't treat me any worse than they have done already. It's the only way we're going to find anything out, isn't it?"

"I suppose so," said Helen.

"While I'm gone, you can look at the pictures under the microscope – they're in my travelling clock, remember. And don't lose that piece of paper, for heaven's sake! It's all we've got left, thanks to me!"

"Good luck!" whispered Helen. She made sure Sam could

still get into the cottage, then she slipped away into the darkness. Sam watched her from the gate until she signalled 'OK', then went in at the back door and carefully closed it. It was the sort that locked itself and only needed a key to open it.

Sam took a deep breath and crept towards the curtained room. Gingerly, he tried the handle, but this time the door was locked.

"I hope it's not bolted from inside!" he said to himself.

From his pocket he took one of the keys that Helen's cousin had made. He had put them in different pockets so that they didn't jingle against each other.

It wasn't that one. He tried another, and it worked. His most dangerous moment had arrived. He very carefully eased open the door, then closed it again. There was no sound from the sleeping figure on the settee. Sam re-locked the door and flashed his torch around inside the room. Carefully, he eased himself down under the dining table behind two big cardboard boxes. He had just enough space under the table to lie straight out against the wall without being seen.

He switched off his torch, turned slightly on to his side, and went quickly off to sleep. His one hope was that he didn't snore like Uncle Black.

First it was the sound of footsteps on the stairs; then the crash of crockery in the kitchen; then feet thumping up the stairs again. When at last the sound of a key being turned in a lock upstairs filtered through the ceiling, Sam was suddenly wide awake.

There was only a dim light in the room, so the light under the table where Sam was hidden was almost nil. He could see by his watch light that it was half-past nine, and he could hear the sounds of the man stirring in the room. A few seconds later he heard the shout from upstairs.

Pandemonium broke loose.

"He's gone!" Uncle Black's voice. "The flaming kid's gone!"

The sound of more doors shutting, furniture being moved, beds lifted up, cupboards opened, cupboards closed again. Feet on the stairs. Now the man in the room getting up and padding slowly to the door in bare feet. Cupboards being searched downstairs, tables being moved. The back door opening, distant sounds in the yard. The man padding back across the room. The perceptible sound of clothing being put on. The back door again, footsteps in the little passage, the key turning in the man's door. Uncle Black's voice.

"He's gone! The perisher's gone!"

"Good riddance!" It was the stranger who spoke for the first time. His voice was light and matter-of-fact. "Does that mean I can talk now?"

"It may be good riddance for you! What about me? I'll have to explain it to his parents!"

Sam, in his cardboard hiding place, was smiling to himself. He knew at last what it was like to be the proverbial fly on the wall.

"He must be around. I thought you said you'd locked him in?"

"I did. I know I did! But he's just disappeared. His window's shut from the inside – it's too far for him to jump, anyway. His door's still locked from the outside, just the way I left it. But the damn kid and his luggage have gone! The room's as tidy as if he'd never been in it."

"He must have pushed the key out of the lock and caught it on a piece of newspaper – you know the old trick."

"No. I turned the key right round when I left it in the lock. He couldn't have pushed it out."

"What did he do, then, go up the chimney?"

"Ha, very funny! How am I going to explain it? How am I going to find the little devil?"

90

"Perhaps you shouldn't have been so harsh."

"Yes – and perhaps you should never have come here. Muddled things nicely, you have."

"Well, you'll have to get me away again, won't you?"

"Is the heat off?"

"How should I know? I haven't been able to listen to the radio with that kid upstairs. You should never have locked him up. He was far less harm when he was snooping around than when he was permanently locked upstairs. I haven't been able to draw breath for fear of giving the game away."

"It was your idea in the first place. No one will ever know, you said. Just a favour for an old school chum, you said."

"You didn't have to accept."

"You were too persuasive. Now you've got me in a mess and I'm already fed up with it. Flaming kid's probably gone back home to sit on his doorstep for two weeks."

Sam hardly dared breathe as there was a pause in the conversation.

"Did you get everything?" said the stranger.

"We can pick up the passport tomorrow night."

"Then I'll go as soon as I've got it."

"Don't you think it's risky? Too early, if you ask me."

"Can't be much riskier than getting mixed up here much longer. You've lost the kid, and you can't exactly tell the fuzz you've lost him until I'm out of it."

"It's your neck."

Again there was a long pause. Then the stranger spoke again.

"Are you sure you checked everywhere?"

"What do you mean?"

"The kid. Where can he have gone to?"

"His luggage has gone as well."

"He could have chucked that in a field somewhere."

"Well, I've checked every place round here that's big enough to hide in. Anyway, there'd be no sense in him escaping just to stick around, would there?"

"S'pose not. What I'm saying is – if the kid's gone, I can stretch my legs and get myself out of this cramped hole. You've no idea what it's like trying to do everything in silence. It was good in a way having the kid locked up, because at least I could use the kitchen and the rest, but it was tough being quiet, I can tell you."

"Well – let's get some breakfast, then."

They went out, leaving the door open. If he listened very carefully, Sam could still hear their conversation. At first, they spoke about ordinary things. Then Sam heard his uncle say, "Any idea what this is?"

"Where'd you get it?"

"The kid had it yesterday. I thought it might be worth something."

"You didn't take it off him? You *have* been treating the poor little blighter badly, haven't you? Let me see it."

Sam strained his ears and practically stopped breathing in case he missed the answer.

"Dunno," said the man. "Just a trinket. Might be diamonds, might be glass. Don't see what it's for. It's got no hooks so it can't be a brooch, or an earring, or something off a charm bracelet. Bit funny, if you ask me. I'd let the kid have it back."

"Bit late."

"That's your problem. But I shouldn't think it's worth hanging on to – not for the fuss."

After that the conversation went on to ordinary questions about breakfast and coffee, and Sam stopped listening. He had already learned most of what he wanted to know: the man needed a passport, and was possibly going the following night. Sam wondered where? With a passport – out of the country, of course, but where?

And the spaceship – his uncle still had it on him – but what would he do with it now? Sam hoped that he wouldn't take it outside and throw it on to the fell in a temper. That way, they'd have no chance of finding it. He just hoped his uncle would keep it long enough for Sam to have the opportunity to steal it back again.

Sam was beginning to feel cramped. While the men were out of the room he stretched himself and changed position, then started to think about his next move. He realised that his uncle wasn't going to come looking for him today – and that was good. It meant he could spend the day at the farmhouse fairly openly, as long as he didn't go anywhere that was visible from Drift Hill.

His immediate problem was how to get out of the room again. He had been prepared to stay all day and into the following night if necessary. He'd brought bits of food in his pockets, just in case. But now that he had learned most of what he wanted to know, he was anxious to get out. He wondered if he could get past the kitchen entrance without being seen, but it seemed too risky. He'd be caught far too easily. He decided to stay for the time being, and hoped that a better opportunity would occur later.

CHAPTER TEN

The Microscope

In the dim light under the table, hemmed in by his cardboard boxes, Sam tried to stretch his cramped legs again. He wondered how Helen was getting on, and if she had looked at the tiny pictures the aliens had drawn. What could the pictures have said?

He knew how difficult it was to talk to an alien, even in pictures. When he had finished his own drawings of the solar system, Sam had run out of ideas. What would the aliens think of? Sam had thought about drawing his house, but couldn't really see how it might help.

His thoughts turned to the men in the kitchen. He wished he knew which way they were facing. If both their backs were to the door, he could make an exit without being seen. But if they weren't. . .

He desperately wanted the little spaceship back, and he was determined he would find it that night. It didn't matter what he had to do to get it. Even if he had to lift up the pillows they were sleeping on, he'd find it.

As he finished these wandering thoughts, his ears picked up the sound of chairs scraping in the kitchen, the men getting up. One set of footsteps went upstairs. Then Sam saw the legs of the stranger coming back into the room. Suddenly their owner called out, "Jeremy. . .!"

There was no reply.

"*Jerem-ee. . .!*" he called again, but still had no reply. The legs left the room and started going up the stairs.

Without waiting to think any more of danger, Sam took his chance. In two seconds he had parted the boxes and squeezed out from under the table. In another two he had left the room and was making for the back door, silent and fast.

Outside, he turned sharp right and headed for the outbuilding. He paused behind it to catch his breath and let his heart slow down.

Sam considered his route back to the farmhouse. He had to do it in a way that was invisible from Drift Hill. It would be ideal if Uncle Black and the other man went out for a while, but Sam knew there was no way the stranger would show his face in daylight.

Recovering his breath, Sam carefully climbed the barbed wire that bordered the field at the back of the old building. He ran along beside an overgrown hedge, where he was out of sight from any windows in the cottage. After four or five hundred metres, the hill dipped down, and the cottage was lost from sight. He pushed his way back through the hedge where it was thin. He came out on to the fell, beyond the point where the road from the cottage met the long straight one. The countryside was too open for safety, so Sam went back through the hedge again. He decided to go right round in the other direction, keeping away from Uncle Black's usual route in the car.

He ran up the far edge of the pasture, then carried on running in an enormous anti-clockwise loop. As long as he kept only the roof of the cottage just in sight, he felt he was safe. Halfway down one field he met a farmer-looking man coming the other way. The man said, "Good morning" and Sam said, "Good morning", but nothing else happened. Eventually, after climbing two dry stone walls, Sam found himself almost half a mile from the cottage to the west. He was nearing the long straight road.

There were several humps in this area, and Sam found that he could keep the cottage out of sight practically all the way until he reached the road. There, he had to chance a quick crossing. Once on the other side, he kept in the ditches and behind such bits of hedge and shrub as he could find.

He arrived at the farmhouse hot and tired.

"Well, look who it is!" said Mrs Wallace as she opened the door. "You've decided to come and see us again, have you?"

"Yes, if it's all right, please," said Sam.

"Of course it's all right. Come in. The children don't often have a friend to play with." She looked at him closely. "Have you had breakfast?"

"Er – no, not yet."

"I see. You got up late and came out in a hurry, I suppose," chuckled Mrs Wallace. "Never mind. I'll fix you up with something really tasty!"

"Thank you," said Sam. "Where are the others?"

"Helen and Jimmy are in Helen's room with the microscope. Why don't you go up and join them, and I'll tell you when your breakfast is ready. How about that?"

"Thank you very much."

Sam whizzed upstairs and met Helen coming out of her room to meet him. Her face shone with excitement, and she was wearing one of the biggest, brightest smiles he'd ever seen on anyone, ever.

"Come on, Sam!" she said. "Quick! Come and have a look!"

"What is it? Hello, Jimmy."

"Hello." At the sight of Sam, Jimmy started jumping up and down. "We can see pictures!"

Before she let Sam have a look through the eyepiece, Helen looked at him with sparkling eyes, and said, "Are you sure you didn't draw these, Sam? I'm just starting to wonder if you've been making things up all along!"

"Don't be silly," said Sam. "Of course I haven't."

"But they can't really have been drawn by. . ." she lowered her voice to a whisper – "something from outer space?"

"What's in them, then? Let me have a look, Helen – please! You know I've been busting to see them since yesterday! It's unfair to keep them away from me any longer."

Helen had only been half-joking, but now she became more business-like.

"Start at this end," she said. She looked through the eyepiece herself and adjusted the little piece of paper. "I think the drawings are in sequence, only they've drawn them from right to left, not left to right."

"Has Jimmy been sworn to secrecy?"

"Yes."

"Good."

Eagerly, Sam leaned over the little microscope. The first drawing he saw was a repeat of his drawing of the solar system, with the figure of Sam standing on the third planet from the sun. He moved the slide along a fraction and saw the second picture, which looked something like this:

"What do you think it is?" said Helen, when she saw Sam move the slide.

"It's the sun again, and the earth again with me standing on it, and – that must be a *real flying saucer* with the *brooch* on top of it! And on top of that, the little thing with three spikes on top and three spikes underneath!"

"Now go on!" said Helen.

"Yes, go on," said Jimmy, who had no intention of being left out. "I've had a look already."

Again, Sam moved the slide the tiniest fraction and saw the image shooting across the eyepiece at high speed. He adjusted it until he was sure he had the next picture in the sequence:

"Got it?" said Helen.

"Yes. The flying saucer is *landing* on the earth. But the little spaceship with the diamonds and the creatures inside is separating from it!"

"You wait until you see the others!" Helen said. She was so excited that Sam found it quite funny and wanted to laugh with excitement himself.

Sam looked at the next picture:

"I see. The flying saucer has landed, and the little spaceship has landed, and *I'm in the middle!*"

"That's right, that's right!"

"It's funny, isn't it?" said Jimmy, laughing himself. Then, unprompted, he started to jump up and down again, which Sam at last realised he always did when he was excited.

"I don't know what the shapes mean, though."

Then Mrs Wallace's voice called up the stairs.

"There's some breakfast for you, Sam! And tell the two elephants to come for a bun and a trunkful of tea, as well!"

Sam looked longingly at the microscope.

"Come on!" said Helen. "Come and have some breakfast. I'm sure you must be starving. We can look at the other fantastic things afterwards!"

"All right," said Sam.

"Oh, Sam, you wait until you see the others!"

"What are they like?"

"Wait until you see," said Helen. "But I don't really understand two of them."

They assembled round the table in the kitchen, where Sam was presented with an enormous cooked breakfast, more like a mixed grill. He ate it with considerable gusto.

"My, you are hungry!" commented Mrs Wallace. "Hasn't your uncle been feeding you?"

The truth was that Sam was very hungry, but he was so anxious to get back and see the remaining drawings that he bolted his food recklessly.

"I shouldn't think it's touching the sides as it goes down," Mrs Wallace commented.

Sam apologised and slowed down for a moment. But he was soon up to full speed again, and finished in no time at all.

Helen and Jimmy had bolted their elevenses as well, and a breathless Helen wiped the tea from her mouth with the back of her hand and said "Come on!" The trio threw several thank yous at Mrs Wallace and bundled back upstairs.

"I don't know. What are they up to?" she said aloud to herself, and laughed.

In Helen's room, Sam put his eye back to the microscope and looked at the next picture. It was drawn like this:

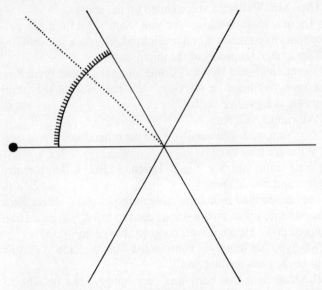

"That's a funny one," said Sam. "It's just a sort of star shape with a knob on the end and a dotted line."

"It looks a bit like a shooting star. That's one of the ones I don't understand."

"I don't understand that one, either," said Jimmy, very seriously.

"Let me see the next one," said Sam.

The next drawing was even stranger:

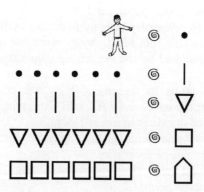

"Well! There's me, and lots of shapes. I don't know what they mean, though."

"The next one's the last one," said Helen. "You wait!"

Sam adjusted the slide once more, and this is what he saw:

"It's me again – carrying the little spaceship to the flying saucer!"

"That's what they want us to do, Sam!" Helen was dancing round and round. "That's what they want us to do! They want us to take them back to their spaceship!"

"Of course!" Sam felt like laughing and crying at the same time. "So we *did* see a spaceship go over the hill that night! And the little spaceship was just a piece of it!"

Sam had another look through the microscope.

"Let's draw them bigger," he said, suddenly. "Come on!"

Helen found some paper, and they copied all of the drawings on to separate pieces as faithfully as they could. Jimmy tried to help, but his drawings were not quite up to the standard required by the organising committee of Helen and Sam.

"If they want us to find their flying saucer for them, they've got to tell us *where it is*," said Sam, when they had the big finished drawings in front of them.

"That means," said Helen, picking up Sam's lead, "they've got to tell us the *direction* it's in. . ."

"That's it!" said Sam. "Look at this star thing! I bet it's a magnetic compass point!"

"But it's got *six* points," said Helen. "A compass only has four points."

"Daft! *Our* compass has four points. Why shouldn't theirs have six? We have longitude and latitude: they might have longitude, leftitude and rightitude for all we know."

"It does sound daft, but I see what you mean."

"You can bet the one with the knob on is magnetic north," Sam went on "– and the dotted line is the angle from north where we can find the other spaceship."

"Look! The dotted line is on the drawing where you're standing between the saucer and the little ship."

"So that means that the next picture is the *distance*," said Sam. "So the symbols on the picture where I'm standing on the dotted line must mean the distance. But how do we know how far each symbol is supposed to be?"

Jimmy had lost interest, and was folding the spare sheets of paper into aeroplanes. Helen and Sam stared at the picture with symbols on and tried to understand it.

"Everything's in sixes, like their compass," said Helen. "They've even got six limbs – three at the top and three at the bottom."

Sam was still thinking.

"I'm going to get a map," said Helen suddenly, and ran

downstairs. Minutes later she came back with a pink ordnance survey map of the area. She started to spread it out over the floor. She looked at the top of the map and found where true north and magnetic north were marked. Armed with a ruler, she then drew a pencil line, starting from Drift Hill Cottage, going along a line in the direction of magnetic north. She had difficulty getting the angle just right, but after double checking she was satisfied.

"How are you getting on with the distance, Sam?"

"Not very far."

"Ha! Funny joke! I'm doing the angle."

"Good," said Sam absent-mindedly.

Helen looked through the microscope again to check the position of the dotted line. Using a fine needle she carefully counted the marks between the pair of compass points, and found that there were thirty-five – giving thirty-six sections. The dotted line passed through the twenty-fifth section.

"They have two-hundred and sixteen degrees in a circle," said Helen out loud to Sam. "Six times six times six."

"Sixes again," said Sam, ducking to avoid one of Jimmy's paper aeroplanes.

Helen concentrated on her map. Using her trigonometry set, she drew another pencil line starting at Drift Hill Cottage. She drew it at the same angle from magnetic north as the line in the drawing, or twenty-five two-hundred-and-sixteenths east of the north line.

"It's forty one and two-thirds degrees," she said to Sam. "Almost north-east."

Sam was still puzzling over the distance diagram.

"If you check this for me," Helen went on, "we can both have a look at the distance problem."

Sam broke out of his thoughts, checked through what Helen had done, and approved it.

"So the flying saucer lies somewhere along that line," said Sam. "But how far? It could be a hundred miles for all we know, unless we can solve this problem."

"It's difficult, isn't it?"

"See the diagram? There's one of me; then there's a squiggle; then there's a dot."

"But the squiggle is on each line, so we can ignore that," said Helen. "It might be a sort of equals sign."

"Genius!" said Sam, lighting up. "Not *might* be, *must* be! What a genius you are!"

"Good," said Helen, delighted. "That means we *can* ignore them, then."

"So ONE SAM *equals* a dot! SIX DOTS *equal* a line! SIX LINES *equal* a triangle; SIX TRIANGLES *equal* a SQUARE—"

"Look, Sam! A square has four corners, and it's the FOURTH shape! And a triangle is the THIRD shape!"

"Yes! And six squares equal a pentagon, which is the next shape up!"

"Only trouble is," said Helen, her face falling, "what do they mean by a Sam equalling one dot?"

Sam suddenly smacked his forehead.

"We're idiots!" he shouted. "How *tall* am I?"

"How should I know?"

"I'm a hundred and sixty centimetres! They must have measured me!"

Suddenly, Sam was doing calculations on the edge of the large piece of paper.

"Listen," he said at last. "Six of *me* is 9.6 metres, which is six dots, which *equals* a line. Six lines are a triangle, which is 57.6 metres. Six triangles are 345.6 metres, which is a square. And six squares are a pentagon, which is 2,073.6 metres!"

"Oh dear!" said Helen. "On this dotted line from the little spaceship to the flying saucer, there are three pentagons, one square, and one triangle."

"Quick! Add them up!"

"That's 2,073.6 plus 2,073.6 plus 2,073.6 plus 345.6 plus

57.6 metres! Which is. . . 6,624 metres!"

"Hooray!" said Sam.

"Boo! That's just over four miles."

Sam jumped up.

"Come on, then," he said. "Let's go! Where's the map?"

"It's here."

"What's the scale?"

"1 to 50,000."

"So we have to measure. . . a line. . . that is... 6,624 divided by 50,000, which is... 0.13248 metres, or 13.248 centimetres away from Drift Hill Cottage!"

Helen measured the distance along the last line she had drawn, and marked it with a cross.

"So that's where the spaceship is!" she said.

Before they had time to enjoy the luxury of having solved a difficult problem, Jimmy made a scary announcement from the window.

"Old Shoutbum's coming!"

Sam and Helen jumped to their feet in panic and rushed to the window. Sure enough, Uncle Black's battered car was stopped on the straight road opposite Fell Farm. Sam's uncle had climbed out and was a quarter of a mile away, walking across the grass towards the farmhouse.

"Come on!" said Sam. "Let's go and find that flying saucer – and quick!"

Without a word of discussion or argument, Sam and Helen gathered up everything they might need: the drawings, the compass, pencils, the trigonometry set, a ruler. Sam carefully put the tiny piece of paper in his travelling clock, closed it, and pushed it into his pocket. They gathered torches, a thin blanket, the map, and threw them into a plastic carrier bag.

Jimmy was sworn to silence and told to stay behind.

Even as they heard the front door bell ringing, Sam and Helen slipped out of the back door and ran east until they came to a deep ditch. They hurled themselves into it, and stayed there, watching.

They saw Mrs Wallace going into the outbuildings of the farm, calling.

CHAPTER ELEVEN

The Spaceship

Much later, they saw Uncle Black's car driving away again.

"What will your mum say if we just go?" said Sam.

"I shan't tell her."

"You must. She'll be worried."

"But if I go back and tell her she might stop me going."

"Why don't you go back and leave a note?"

"I could tell Jimmy what to say."

"No. She might see you."

Helen hesitated.

"All right. I'll go and tell her," she said. "I'm sure she'll be all right. She lets me go off on my own quite a lot. It's okay in this area."

"I'll wait here," said Sam. "I won't go until you're back. And if your mum won't let you come now, I'll wait for you until tonight. It wouldn't be fun to go and find the spaceship without you."

"Okay. Thanks."

Helen left all the equipment with Sam and ran back to the farmhouse.

It was midday. There were only a few wispy clouds in the sky, and the sun was getting hot. Sam closed his eyes and lay on his back in the dry ditch. As he grew hotter, he became drowsy, and went to sleep again. Helen had to wake him up twenty minutes later to show him what she had brought.

"Mum said 'yes'! And she's packed us a big bag for our lunch and tea!" she said.

"Great!" said Sam, getting up. "Let's have some now."

"No. I think we should get right out of your uncle's way first. Mum said he came looking for you. He didn't say you'd run away, or anything, so Mum doesn't know you have. But he wanted to know where you were. He told Mum he hadn't seen you all morning. Mum told him you were here earlier, but that you must have gone off with me."

"What did he say to that?"

"He told Mum to tell you as soon as you were back, to go straight home to the cottage."

"What did you tell your mum about me disappearing?"

"I told her that he was cross with you, and that you didn't want to go back until tonight. That was when I asked her if we could take a picnic and go for a long hike."

"Good. That's really good."

"Let's look at the map, shall we, and plan our route?"

They circumnavigated Drift Hill to the south-east and east and gradually made their way back towards the line that Helen had drawn on the map. When they reached the line, they were roughly a mile north-east of the cottage. Then they stopped for lunch.

Sam handed out food while Helen spread out all the papers and started doing more calculations.

"The twenty-five units out of their two hundred and sixteen units for a circle is the same as forty-one and a bit degrees east from magnetic north," she said.

"Have a salmon sandwich," said Sam.

"The distance given is 6,624 metres from Drift Hill Cottage; or 4,140 Sams laid end-to-end." Helen laughed, and won a smile from Sam. "So – if they've mis-measured you by just one centimetre, the distance could be wrong by 41.4 metres either way."

"Have another salmon sandwich."

"Thank you. Now. The circumference of a circle with a

radius of 6,624 metres is roughly. . . 41,600 metres. And as each of their 'degrees' is a two-hundred-and-sixteenth of a circle, that means an error of one of their degrees at that distance is 41,600 divided by two hundred and sixteen, which is. . . just over two hundred metres. That means it could be two hundred metres on either side of us."

"I didn't know you were a mathematical genius as well as an ordinary one," said Sam.

"There's no such thing as an *ordinary* genius, Sam. I just like trigonometry and map-reading, that's all."

"Don't you like salmon sandwiches?"

"Sorry, I'll eat them now. I just wanted to work out what sort of error we might find when we get there."

"Ah! You like trigonometry sandwiches!"

"Ha, ha!"

"Where does the 'X' fall on the map?" said Sam. "I never had a chance to look with Uncle Black coming down and trying to interfere."

Helen pointed.

"It's right on the beck coming down through that hill."

"Is that what you call a river – a beck?"

"Well, a stream, yes."

"So what you're saying is – have a cucumber sandwich, they're delicious – when we get to the 'X' on the map, we should be within two hundred metres of the spaceship in any direction?"

"Thank you – yes, if all our calculations are correct."

"You did most of them," said Sam.

"No. Joint effort."

They lay in the grass and finished their meal, then packed their bags and set off again. They were both tired, but the exhilaration of being so close to a real UFO was more than enough to keep them going.

They had put a little mark on Helen's compass at forty-one degrees east. By keeping the needle where north was shown,

109

they were able to walk roughly in the direction of the mark. The countryside was very hilly. It would have been easier on their legs to walk around the contours, but they found it more fun to follow the line straight as much as they could.

They came to a farm after another two miles. They had to deviate slightly to walk round it, but referring to the map brought them quickly back on to the correct line.

As they travelled further north-east, they climbed higher and higher until the grassland – the fell – became poorer and poorer. When they reached the shoulder of a long ridge, they saw the beck for the first time, down below them on the far side.

They kept faithfully to the compass, and it brought them nearer and nearer to the long crease that had been carved by the running water over thousands of years.

"The only trouble is," said Sam, "we don't know exactly how far we've walked. It's much more difficult to identify where we are in this sort of place, with no real landmarks."

"We can check where we are with the compass," said Helen. "As long as we can see a couple of peaks. Look – there's one there, and another one over there."

They sat down on the fell and spread the map on their knees. Helen showed Sam how to take two compass bearings, draw them on the map, and see where they met.

"That's where we are!" said Helen at last. "It looks as though we should be down towards the beck a bit more to be back on our line."

Having to go more towards the stream meant that they were nearer to their destination than they had thought.

"As soon as we have to cross the beck, we're about a hundred metres from our target!" said Helen.

They were going downhill now, faster and faster towards the water. They finally reached it at a point that was relatively easy to cross. They continued up the other side. Now they were looking all around, everywhere, trying to see what they had come so far to find. They stopped when they had walked the last hundred metres, climbing again. They turned to look back at where they had come.

"We ought to mark this spot," said Sam.

"What with? There aren't any branches because there aren't any trees."

"We'll leave our bags here."

"Okay."

They piled their bags up so that they were visible from a distance, then set out to comb the area around them. They searched for over an hour, walking up to a quarter of a mile in each direction. They spread out so that they could cover more ground between them than by staying together.

It was Sam who saw it first. He noticed something lying in the coarse grass several hundred metres away, glinting in the sunshine.

"Helen!" he shouted.

Helen came running, shouting as she ran.

"Have you seen it? Have you seen it, Sam?!"

"There's something down there!" He pointed. As Helen reached him, she looked, and they both ran down the fell together. They held hands to keep their balance, running almost faster than their legs would let them go. They screamed with laughter as they went, nearer and nearer, faster and faster.

They arrived breathless and too excited to speak, and gazed at the strange object in total astonishment.

It was less than a metre in length – perhaps seventy centimetres – but it wasn't like a saucer at all. It was more like a boat, or a flattened cigar. Its sides were encrusted, not with diamonds, but with emeralds. The grass for several metres to the south-west was scorched.

They stared in fascination at the colour of the metal. It showed such variations in the bright light that it was almost impossible to say what colour it really was. It was truly

111

iridescent, sometimes purple, sometimes blue or green, shimmering in the sun.

On top was a slot, just big enough to hold the little "brooch" that they had found. All around were tiny holes, and the entire object was so finely engineered with its tiny details that it took their breath away to see it.

"It's beautiful!" Helen breathed at last.

"Just look!" was all Sam could say.

"Let's pick it up and take it back to base."

They both knelt reverently beside it and tried its weight. It was heavy, but not too heavy. Carefully holding it between them, they carried it triumphantly back to where they had left their bags.

"We've got to hide it," said Sam, serious now.

"Why?"

"It's too valuable."

"What do you mean?"

"You saw how much of an interest Uncle Black took in the little ship with diamonds in. This one is covered in emeralds. Whatever it is, Helen, it's priceless. If anyone sees us with it, they'll be as amazed as we were, but they'll get it taken away from us. Honest."

"Yes. I see what you mean."

They were halfway home by now. They had stopped to rest and have some more food and drink. Sam had carried the spaceship most of the way, under one arm, while Helen carried the bags.

"If anyone finds out it's a spaceship, the government will want it. They'll probably blow it up or something."

"Do you think so, really?"

"Yes. They can't trust it, you see. They'll think it's full of dangerous microbes, or something."

"It might be."

"I don't care. They're our friends now."

112

"What if someone stops us on the way back?"

"That's what started to worry me. I think we ought to disguise it. And I've *got* to get the little spaceship from Uncle Black tonight. I've *got* to! Now that we've found this one, we can't let them down. We've got to put them back together again!"

"We can put the plastic carrier bag over one end—"

"And my jumper over the other! I'll just carry it as if it's in the carrier bag."

"What are we going to do with it back at the farm? Is it too risky to take it up into the hay loft?"

"It's either that, or we'll have to bury it somewhere. Burying it would be horrible."

"All right. We'll hide it under the straw, then."

They rearranged their luggage, then set off again. As they neared Drift Hill, they circled widely towards the east again, the way they had come. They soon reached the road far enough east to be out of sight of the cottage.

But as soon as they started to cross the road, they realised that they weren't out of sight of Uncle Black. His car was stopped on the brow of the hill that hid the cottage from view. He was waiting where he could see the countryside for the greatest distance all round.

At the same moment that Sam and Helen saw the car half a mile away, Uncle Black must have seen them. Their hearts almost stopped as they recognised the dreaded sound that echoed thinly across the hills around them. It was the sound of the car's engine starting.

CHAPTER TWELVE

The Move

By the time Zambel had finished copying the message from the piece of paper on to the bio-screen, he had decided on his response. The best thing to do was simply to copy what the giant had written.

It was still dark outside. Armed with a bio-computer copy of what he had keyed in, Zambel opened the hatch and stepped on to the fairly smooth flat surface on which the capsule was now standing. He approached the sheet, which to him was like a huge billboard fifteen centimetres thick. He drew at the bottom of it, as high as he could reach, an exact copy of what he had seen from the capsule. Then he went back inside and at last found some sleep.

When it was light again, the board disappeared for a long time. Zambel told Lam and Mogon what he had done, and they approved his action.

When the second board appeared, they gathered round a porthole to look.

"The giant has created an image of itself!" said Lam.

Zambel thought for only a moment.

"Then we shall give it an image of us!" he said.

The giant was motionless when Lam went outside and drew a large picture of a Zargan, and returned.

It was a long time before the giant responded again, but this time the excitement of the Zargans grew.

"It has shown itself standing on its planet," said Mogon. "The circle with dashes round it must be its representation of its sun."

"And look!" said Lam. "It has represented one of the giant

red horses with our bolt in its side! And it has copied our image of ourselves standing by it!"

"This seems to leave no doubt that we are dealing with the intelligence of this planet," said Zambel. "And if that is the case, we must respond with a message that will get us out of our difficulties."

"Where is the giant now?" said Lam.

Mogon, who was near a porthole, looked out.

"He is lying horizontally and without motion," he said drily, "like the great mountains of Zarg."

"What we need to do," said Zambel, "is to ask the giant to find the Ark for us."

The other two greeted his suggestion with admiration.

"But how can we do such a thing?" they said, almost simultaneously.

"We have already learned," Zambel went on, "that we can represent ourselves and the giant. We now need to show the giant what happened to us, and how we became separated from our mother ship. Then we need to show the giant what we want it to do. And we must devise a method of telling the giant exactly where the Ark lies, both in direction and distance. I am sure that we can use the magnetic field of the planet to do this. And we already know the distance, from our bio-computer calculations."

"The only measurement we have in common knowledge," said Lam, "is the length of the giant itself."

"Excellent, Lam. You must take some readings from outside while the giant is motionless, and Mogon and I shall devise a method of conveying our ideas on the board."

Much later, the giant still had not moved, but the Zargans' messages had been written on the huge board as large as they could make them.

But before the giant moved again, they were suddenly subjected to the terrible sickening movements that they had had to withstand on previous occasions. As far as they could tell, they were in the hands of another giant.

The movements continued for some time, while the three of them clung to the sides of the capsule to avoid being injured. Shortly afterwards, everything went dark again. Apart from the occasional acceleration and deceleration forces, they seemed to be trapped in a black world of the unknown, with no one daring to take the risk of leaving the capsule.

Apart from a brief period of light, approximately one of the planet's days later, they had no clue as to what was happening, but they sent the confirmation signal to the Ark to remain sealed for another day.

The first change in their situation appeared half a planet-day later.

Lam had been watching the bio-panel. He was checking that the information coming from the Ark was satisfactory, and that no problems had developed. He suddenly became excited.

"Zambel! Mogon! Look!"

His two colleagues joined him at the screen, and he indicated the statistical review sequences that were constantly unfolding whenever there was a change.

"The Ark is coming closer!" he said. "It is moving at a rate of six thousand kilometres an hour – possibly the locomotive speed of the giants."

"I wonder if our giant has read our messages, or if the ship has been located by another giant and is being taken for examination?" said Zambel. "Power up the remote external sensors on the Ark."

Lam passed a hand over the pulse pad, and it displayed a confirmation of the powering-up sequence. Shortly afterwards, statistics began to fill the screen.

"Everything is functioning normally. There has been no interference with the Ark's locks," Lam reported. "If there is any interference, we must be prepared to send a signal to unseal the biosphere and to release the future generations of Zargans on to the planet."

"If there is any interference," said Mogon, "it may already be too late. By then, the ship may be inside a laboratory in a sealed environment. We should release them now."

"There is a simple way to compromise," suggested Lam. "It is possible to set the seals to release if the sensors detect the presence of more artificial light than sunlight."

"An excellent compromise, Lam," said Zambel. "See that it is done. But let us hope that the Ark is in the hands of *our* giant. I'm afraid I do not believe that releasing our people on to this planet will ensure the survival of our race for very long."

Zambel looked across the control room.

It was still dark outside the diamond panes.

CHAPTER THIRTEEN

The Chase

"You go!" shouted Helen. *"I'll take the spaceship!"*

Each second was vital, and Sam didn't stop to waste a single one. He pushed his precious parcel into Helen's arms and ran up the fell the way they had come down.

Helen didn't waste any seconds either, but carried on across the road at full speed towards the farm.

"He can't chase us both," she thought as she ran. "And anyway, it's Sam he wants, not me."

Luckily for Sam, his uncle's car didn't start first go, so Sam gained a few precious seconds. He also discovered that it takes nearly a minute for an old car to travel half a mile from a standing start, including stopping again. In that minute, Sam was nearly a quarter of a mile away from the road. He didn't stop to look as he heard the car screeching to a halt, nor when the door banged as his uncle scrambled out and started after him up the slope.

Sam, however, had another factor in his favour. Sam might have guessed, but didn't think of it at the time. He knew his Uncle Black was an extremely lazy person, but it also meant he was not much use at running up hills. So by the time another minute had passed, Sam was further away from his uncle than when the car had stopped.

When Sam did glance back, his uncle was standing still, holding his sides. He was cursing Sam and everything within earshot, which was mostly grass.

Sam, unable to contain his emotions, put a thumb to his nose and waggled his fingers at his uncle. For good measure, he poked out his tongue.

He didn't want to leave anything to chance, so he ran further up the fell until he saw his pursuer turn and walk painfully back to his car and slam the door. Then, to Sam's horror, he saw the car turn off the road on to the fell and start driving up the hill, bouncing and skidding its way up towards him.

In panic for the second time in a few minutes, Sam ran again, this time looking for places where a car couldn't go. There was a ditch running straight down the slope to his right and he made for that. He crossed it, and carried on running round the contour of the hill. Behind him he could hear the car whining and revving.

He glanced over his shoulder. The car was still a quarter of a mile away, but it had just found the ditch in front of it, and Sam's uncle was driving up and down trying to find a way across.

Then the car went madly down the hill. It turned back on to the road, past the ditch, and started up the hill once more, on Sam's side of it. As soon as he realised what was happening, and with some of his breath back, Sam turned and ran towards the ditch. He climbed slightly as well, to take himself further away from the road. Again he crossed it, and again ran along the contour to give himself an easy run. When he was two hundred metres from the ditch, he started straight up the hill.

Suddenly, Sam realised what his uncle was doing. He had driven the car on up the hill next to the ditch, much higher than Sam was now, and was climbing out. Now he was running down the hill towards Sam, which was a lot easier with his unfit body.

Sam decided to continue running on the contour. He waited until his uncle had dropped down the hill far enough to be at the same height, then Sam switched to running up hill again. He saw his uncle, already flagging, trying to run up after him, then give up. He was still the vital two hundred metres away, and he was finished.

"You wait until I get hold of you, Sam Johnson!" he

shouted. Even his shout was short of breath, and he sat down heavily on the grass and lay flat.

Sam glanced back only once more, then continued to run on up the hill.

Sam found a line of wind-bent trees that gave him a lofty view of Drift Hill Cottage and the farm. He sat down with his back against a trunk to regain his breath and decide his next move.

One thing he did know was that he had to get the little spaceship back from his uncle, whatever the risk. The only time he could do it was at night. He cursed himself for not searching more thoroughly before, when he'd had the opportunity.

He realised that he couldn't search without a torch, and now his torch was at the farm. He'd have to go back to the farm to get it, but he didn't dare go anywhere near while his uncle was still on the rampage. He would have to wait until dark, whatever.

Reaching this conclusion, Sam realised how tired he was and lay down and went to sleep.

When he woke up again the stars were out and he was cold. A light, cool breeze was blowing, and the black hills were huddled against the sky. He looked at his watch and was horrified to see that it was three o'clock in the morning. He only had his shirt on top, and it was probably the drop in temperature that had woken him up. He climbed to his feet straight away. There was enough of a moon to see by, and he started running down to the farm.

When he arrived he went straight up into the hay loft and found his torch. His first surprise was to see Helen fast asleep in the hay. He didn't want to wake her up, so he wrote a note saying that he was going "into the lion's den."

Time was too short for him to go looking for where Helen

had hidden the big spaceship, so he pulled on a jumper and went straight out again towards the cottage. He still had all the keys in separate pockets, so he knew he wouldn't have any trouble getting in.

The cottage seemed even more frightening when Sam stood outside the back door feeling for the right key. He knew he was walking into trouble, but he was so afraid that the little spaceship might get lost forever that he was prepared to run whatever risks it took to get it back.

Silently, he turned the key and slipped inside. It was a quarter to four by now, and he knew that there wasn't very much darkness left. He went straight up to his uncle's room and searched everywhere while his uncle snored. He looked through all his uncle's pockets, all his drawers, and even dared to push his hand under his pillow and gently sweep it around to see if the spaceship was there. But it wasn't.

He went down to the kitchen and looked in all the drawers and cupboards there. He looked in the wellington boots by the back door, and on all the ledges he could find. He searched the dining-room drawers and every conceivable place he could think of. But he didn't find it.

At last he decided to search the stranger's room. He turned the handle as quietly as he could and went in. The other man didn't snore like his uncle, so he couldn't be sure that he was asleep. But Sam looked carefully at him and was satisfied by the quiet rhythm of his breathing and the peaceful look on his face. Again, Sam searched his pockets and all the odd places where it might have been hidden. He looked for fifteen minutes more until it started getting light outside.

He realised with a sinking heart that he no longer had any hope of finding it that night. The only chance he had left was to listen to their conversation again as he had the previous morning, hoping beyond reason that one of them would mention it again. And the only safe place in the house was under the table behind the cardboard boxes.

Feeling very, very tired, Sam opened the channel between the boxes and slipped quietly under the table. He moved the boxes back, settled himself down, and again was overcome by an irresistible desire to sleep.

It seemed to Sam that he had spent most of his stay in Cumbria so far waking up to strange situations. He found the following morning to be no exception.

According to his watch, it was eleven o'clock. The room was wide open and someone was knocking incessantly on the back door. Between attacks, he could hear a woman's shrill voice penetrating the walls and the woodwork, demanding to be let in.

"It's no good pretending there's no one there!" it said. "I saw you through the kitchen window!"

Sam realised with interest that it was the old lady from the train.

"I haven't come all this way just to be locked out!" she shouted. The rapping and banging restarted with renewed vigour. "I shall hammer on this door until you let me in!"

It occurred to Sam that his uncle must be out. The only reason why the door wasn't being answered was because the stranger didn't want to show his face to anyone.

"If you don't open the door immediately, I shall start breaking windows!" shrilled the voice.

Sam almost laughed out loud when half a minute later he heard, "Well, I warned you!" followed by the sound of breaking glass. Then he heard the sound of feet in the hall outside the room and the stranger's voice saying "Right, that's it! I'll get the police on you!"

"Don't threaten me, young man! If you don't open this door, I shall break more windows until you do!"

At last the back door was opened. Sam heard what sounded like a small whirlwind, and the old lady was inside the cottage and swishing around it looking into the rooms.

"Are you Jeremy Black?" she said.

There was a pause.

"Well? Are you, or aren't you?"

The man decided that he was.

"Yes, I am," he said.

"Where's the boy, then?"

Sam realised that the stranger had made his third mistake in claiming that he was Jeremy Black. The first was being seen at the window, and the second was opening the door and letting the woman in.

"Er – boy?"

"Sam Johnson!" snapped the woman. "I've come to see him. Where is he?"

"He's. . . out."

"Out where?"

"Just – out."

"Are you responsible for this child, or not? I have come all the way from Carlisle – in my own car – to talk to you about the boy and see how he's getting on, and you don't even know where he is! Are you in charge of him for three weeks, or aren't you?"

"In. . . what?" said the man.

"I take back all I've said about the current generation!" snapped the woman. "The one before it and after mine seems to be composed entirely of gibbering imbeciles!"

"Why don't you mind your own business and clear off?" said the man.

"I spoke to the boy the other day, and he said he was locked in his room. Is that true?"

"No, it isn't true. He's always telling lies, that boy."

"Saints preserve us, of course he's always telling lies – that's why he's here, isn't it?"

"Is it?" The man sounded confused. Then he suddenly seemed to find some confidence. "Look, lady, he's not here, and you're not welcome, so will you just shove off and leave

123

me in peace?"

"I will not 'shove off' as you so crudely put it, until I have seen the boy. I have had no peace of mind since learning that he had been *locked away*, and I didn't come all the way back just to be told to 'shove off'!"

The man had had enough nonsense.

"If you don't shove off now, I'll shove you off!" he said.

Sam hadn't found a conversation so exhilarating in his whole life before. He wondered what the outcome would be.

"Don't speak to me like that!" said the lady. "This umbrella is good enough to break windows, and it's good enough to break your head!"

"Oh, it is, is it?"

This was beginning to sound more menacing, and Sam started to worry. There was a short silence now, and Sam wondered what was happening. Were they just looking at each other?

"I've decided to go after all," the lady said.

"Oh, you have, have you?"

"I don't know what you've done with the boy, but I think the police might be interested."

"You just come back here. . ."

"You wanted me to leave two seconds ago. You don't seem to be able to make up your mind. Perhaps you have an aversion to the police, is that it?"

Suddenly she screamed.

"What are you doing? Get your hands off me, you rogue! I know who you are, and I'll tell the police!"

There were sounds of struggling in the hall and Sam felt frightened. He didn't know what to do. If he joined in the struggle he would be discovered, and probably caught anyway. He didn't think that he and the old lady between them could overpower a grown man. But if he kept quiet, he would have a chance of rescuing her or getting help. He decided to keep quiet.

Meanwhile, the struggle was continuing. He heard a clatter on the floor – possibly the woman's umbrella being thrown down.

"I'll teach you to break windows!" shouted the man.

"I know who you are, and you're not Jeremy Black!" said the old lady. "I've seen your picture in the newspapers! I've got a very good memory, you see, *Mr Charlie Fenwick!*"

There was another short silence.

"Put that away!" said the lady's voice.

"I'm afraid you've said too much, lady. Now, if you don't do as I say, I'll shoot! There's no one hereabouts to hear the noise, so don't get any brave ideas!"

"Well! That just about confirms that you're Charlie Fenwick, doesn't it? Escaped from an open prison three days ago, if I recall, and thought to have gone abroad! Well, well!"

"Upstairs!" A barked command.

"Very well. But my sister will miss me! She knows where I am!"

"I shouldn't worry, lady. I don't intend to stick around that long."

The sound of the steps receded up the stairs, and Sam breathed a sigh of relief. He was glad he hadn't interfered, and glad that the lady hadn't been hurt. If the man had a gun, there was certainly nothing that he, Sam, could have done.

Suddenly, helping the old lady and bringing Charlie Fenwick to justice were more important than recovering the little spaceship. He realised that the man would probably be upstairs for several minutes, perhaps tying the old lady up and gagging her. He seized his opportunity to escape from under the table and out of the cottage. He would run down to the farm and they could drive into the village and alert the authorities straight away. It seemed strange to Sam not to be able to pick up a telephone and call them.

He scrambled out and ran round towards the outbuildings. The last thing he wanted, he told himself, was to meet his uncle coming in at the side gate. He worked his way down the hedge and then went through it towards the road. There was no one coming and he started to run down the hill as fast as he could to the farm.

But as he ran, he realised that his luck had run out. His uncle's car appeared suddenly over the brow of the hill coming from the village. Sam had nearly reached the long straight road, but his uncle, seeing him, accelerated and aimed the vehicle in Sam's direction, closing the gap between them at breakneck speed. Sam turned this way and that like a frightened, cornered rabbit as the car mounted the fell and came straight towards him. Wherever he ran, the car turned. This time, there was nowhere the car couldn't go.

As it came within three metres and slid to a halt, Sam made a last petrified effort to escape. But his uncle was fresh, and Sam was already tired from running.

In the final dash for freedom, Sam lost.

CHAPTER FOURTEEN

The Rescue

Sam didn't try to struggle when the big grip clamped on his arm. His uncle led him firmly to the car and put him in the passenger seat. To Sam's surprise – and much to his relief – his uncle didn't seem very angry. He just behaved as if other things were on his mind that were more important. Collecting Sam was just a minor nuisance like getting the washing in when it was raining, or letting a bee out of the window.

"Where have *you* been?" said Uncle Black.

Sam didn't say anything at first. His uncle slumped wearily into the driver's seat and put the car into gear.

"You're a damn nuisance, that's what you are."

Sam still remained silent.

"Well? Answer me. Where have you been?"

"I slept up on the hill," Sam said at last, with perfect truth.

"Is that where your luggage is?"

Sam didn't want to implicate the farm in any way.

"Yes," he said. He knew it was a lie, but it didn't seem to matter, lying to Uncle Black. He felt no twinges of guilt.

Uncle Black set the car in motion and steered it over the bumpy grass down towards the road.

"Well, you'll have to do without it for a bit. I'm not going up to get it—"

Sam had visions of his breathless uncle climbing the hill.

" – and I can't let you run off again, either. You shouldn't have gone off in the first place. You shouldn't have come here, should you? Your mum and dad won't be happy if I tell them about you hiding the letter."

Sam felt his courage returning.

"They won't be happy if I tell them about you locking me up, will they?" he said.

"You shouldn't have gone snooping when I told you not to. That was bad."

"I didn't do any harm," said Sam. Then, daringly: "I only wanted to know why that room was locked."

He saw his uncle give him a quick sideways glance.

"Well," – and suddenly his uncle was a changed man, actually trying to be nice – "you can have the run of the house after today, because I'll be going away tonight. I'll be back in the morning."

No, you won't, thought Sam. *Not when we get to the cottage and you find out what's been happening with the old lady, you won't.*

"I'll open up that old dark room downstairs – there's nothing much in there. You can use it as your own, if you like, during the day. I'll do that this evening, before I go. How about that?"

"Thank you," said Sam politely. Then, as the car turned up the hill towards the cottage again, he added suddenly, "Can I have my brooch back, please?"

His uncle seemed confused for a moment, then remembered.

"You're very keen to have that brooch, aren't you?" he said. "Where did you find it?"

"It's mine. I've always had it."

Just the faintest trace of a fatherly smile crossed Uncle Black's lips for a moment.

"You found it in my garden, behind the outbuildings, you little fibber."

Sam didn't answer. They were approaching the cottage now. Suddenly the old lady's parked car came into view, and Sam waited for the storm to break. He thought again of escape, but didn't think much of his chances. His uncle stopped the car, climbed out and led him by the arm round the cottage to the back. There was a strange look on his face.

"Hey! Someone's broken a window!" Uncle Black turned accusingly to Sam. "Was that you?"

"No!" Sam protested. "I don't know anything about it. I wasn't even here."

"Yes, you were. You were running down from the cottage when I came over the hill, you little liar."

"It wasn't me!"

"We'll see about that."

Sam made a last desperate bid for what he wanted more than anything else in the world.

"Can I please just have my brooch? I promise I won't bother you any more. I'll go and stay on the hill, or in your outbuilding, or anywhere. I don't care. If you'll just give me the brooch. *Please,* uncle!"

"So that's what you were up to! Trying to break in to steal the brooch, weren't you, you little thief!"

"I wasn't! And I'm not a thief, and I'm not a liar!"

Sam was half-dragged into the back door, but as they got inside, his uncle hesitated. He'd seen the lady's umbrella lying on the floor, and the door to the curtained room wide open. It must have started alarm bells ringing in his uncle's brain.

Now you're going to find out! thought Sam. *Now you're going to see who broke the window!*

Uncle Black stopped, turned, and pushed Sam backwards into the little kitchen.

"Stay there!" he snapped, and closed the door.

Sam's next instinct was to escape again. He turned the handle on the window, but the window was stuck. He looked around it and saw that two screws had been driven into it a long time ago, and painted over. That only left the door, but he didn't dare open it. He hadn't heard his uncle going up the stairs, and he thought he could hear whispering in the hall outside. It was too risky. Instead, he stuffed several biscuits into one pocket and a small apple into the other. In doing it, he realised he still had the keys. What if his uncle searched him?

Changing his mind, he rammed one biscuit into his mouth, and put the others back. He took off one shoe, laid two keys at the bottom, put it back on, then did the same with the other shoe. Then he ate another biscuit. Then another. Finally, he ate the apple.

When his uncle still hadn't returned, he put several more biscuits in one pocket and an orange in the other. Then his uncle opened the door.

"There's a change of plan," he said. The slight trace of preoccupation had disappeared. Instead, he looked deeply shocked.

"Who broke the window, then?" said Sam, deliberately goading him. *Get out of that without giving the game away!* he thought.

"It was an accident. A friend of mine has arrived while I was out. I've had to give him your room for a while. You probably noticed the other car outside."

Very clever, thought Sam. *Now who's a big fibber? And now where are you going to put me?*

"I'm going to put you in my room just for today."

And I know why!

"I'll have to lock you in, but it's only for today. Just as your last punishment, see?"

He must think I'm stupid! thought Sam.

They went upstairs. His uncle started picking up things he needed and throwing them out of his room on to the landing.

"Don't try to climb out of the window," he said. "This one's screwed up, so you won't be able to open it."

"May I please have my brooch, now?" Sam asked again. He wasn't going to give up – ever. He wanted the spaceship,

130

and he wanted to finish the task that the little aliens had given them. He wasn't going to let them down now.

"It's in the car. I'll let you have it before I go."

Sam felt like screaming. It had been in the car all the time! *Why hadn't he thought of looking in the car?*

He felt a sudden overwhelming sense of loss. It wasn't just for the spaceship, either – it was his Aunt Mabel bouncing into his thoughts – what would she think when she came back from Ireland and found her husband missing – or in prison?

As his uncle stood up and started for the door, Sam spoke to him, his mind made up.

"You don't have to go with him," he said gently.

His uncle stopped in mid-stride.

"With who?" he said, ungrammatically.

"You know," said Sam. "The man who's escaped from prison. You don't have to go with him."

Uncle Black turned and stared at his nephew.

"How could you know that?"

Sam stared calmly back.

"I overheard."

While his uncle was readjusting his thoughts, Sam continued.

"If you don't go with him, no one will know you had anything to do with it. The man can drive your car. You can say he stole it."

Uncle Black glared, brewing like a thunderstorm.

"You know too much," he growled.

"If you're caught with him, it'll look bad."

More brooding silence.

"If he takes the car," Sam went on, "you can say you didn't know anything about it. They'll just put him back in prison, then. We can make up a story – we can say he locked us all in the cottage and took the car."

Uncle Black stared at Sam for the last time, then strode out of the room and locked the door. Sam's parting plea, an urgent whisper, penetrated the woodwork.

"If you get caught on the road, tell the police he *forced* you to drive – at *gun point*."

For the next half hour there were lots of noises in the house. Things were moved around the floor, footsteps went in and out of the hall. Through his window, Sam could see Jimmy running towards the farm, but there was no sign of Helen. Soon afterwards, his uncle started loading his car with boxes, suitcases and odds and ends. After that he came upstairs again, unlocked the door, and stood just inside the room holding a piece of washing-line.

"I'm sorry," said Uncle Black, "but I'm going to have to tie you up."

"What for?" said Sam. "I haven't done anything. I was trying to help you!"

"I can't afford to let you escape for a while, Sam, that's all. I'm not coming back tomorrow. I'm sticking with my plans."

"You can't just leave me here on my own!" said Sam.

"What have you got in your pockets?"

"My pockets?"

"Yes, your pockets." His uncle was starting to get impatient. "I want to make sure you haven't got a penknife."

Sam turned out his pockets, biscuits and orange included. He felt pleased that he had safely transferred the keys to his shoes. His uncle, satisfied, started tying Sam's ankles to the chair.

"I'll make sure somebody knows you're here. I'll telephone tomorrow. They'll let you out."

"You didn't give me the brooch," said Sam.

"I'll bring it up before I go."

Next, Sam's hands were tied and lashed to the chair behind his back.

132

"You'll have to leave the back door open," Sam said suddenly. "Otherwise no one will be able to get in tomorrow to rescue us" – he hastily corrected himself – "I mean me."

It was a glaring mistake. His uncle picked it up straight away.

"What do you mean – us?" he demanded. "What else do you know?"

Sam went hot and cold.

"I – I just meant me – I said 'me'. It's just the way I said it. You know—"

His uncle stared for a moment, then shrugged.

"Well, just shut up, then, and don't say anything else."

Sam felt relieved.

"Will you leave the back door open?" he said.

"Yes."

"And you won't forget my brooch?"

"No, no," – impatiently – "don't keep on about it. Don't you think I've got enough on my mind as it is?"

Sam caught his eye and stared at him.

"You don't have to go. I wouldn't tell on you, honest."

"It's not just you, now," said Uncle black grimly. "That's the trouble."

Sam knew whom he meant.

"*She* won't tell on you, either," he said slowly, "if I ask her."

Uncle Black stared.

Suddenly, Sam's hours of torture on the train, listening to the old lady, came rushing into his brain. He remembered everything she had told him about herself and started spewing it out in a monotone, like a parrot.

"*Her name's Miss Baxter and she lives in Carlisle and she's got seven brothers and seven sisters. They're all alive. Five of her children are married and she's got twelve grandchildren and two great-grandchildren. One of her granddaughters is an actress who's been in several films,*

133

and one of her own children is high up in the Bank of England..."

Uncle Black looked shocked, and a strange look passed over his face as he stared back at Sam. Sam was still talking as his uncle stood up and slowly walked out, locking the door and taking away the key.

Shortly afterwards, Sam heard two car doors slamming, the old engine starting up, and the rattle of the car as it raced down the hill. His uncle hadn't brought the brooch up to him, and Sam cried out in despair at the window.

"The spaceship, you stupid uncle! *You've gone off with the spaceship!*"

Only thirty seconds later Sam heard footsteps in the hall downstairs.

"Sam! Sam! Where are you?"

It was Helen's voice, sweet and clear.

Sam, never daring to hope that she would come so quickly, lifted his head and shouted.

"I'm here! Uncle Black's room!"

The sound of Helen's feet came racing up the stairs.

"He's locked the door!"

"I know. I'm tied up. The keys are in my shoe! I'll get them!"

"They've both gone!" said Helen. "Him and the man."

"He's an escaped convict!" yelled Sam through the door. "We've got to stop them! And they've still got the brooch in the car!"

"I've been hiding outside ever since I saw your uncle catch you! I caught Jimmy spying on me and sent him home, naughty boy. He shouldn't be mixed up in this."

"I saw him running home. I wondered where you were."

"Someone else's car is here, too. Whose is it?"

"There's a lady tied up in my room. Miss Baxter. I hope she's all right."

134

Sam started to work out how he could get his shoes off with both ankles and hands tied to the chair. He started to rock the chair back and forth until it fell backwards against the bed.

Helen was calling to the old lady to see if she was all right.

"I think she's okay, Sam! I heard her groan when I shouted."

"Thank goodness."

By a series of shuffles, Sam fell on to his side and managed to hook the heel of his shoes against the side of the chest of drawers. With a lot of effort and wriggling he pulled both shoes off, and with more wriggling tipped them so that the keys spilled out.

"Helen! I'm going to try to push the keys under the door!"

With more shuffling and great physical effort, Sam hooked his toe on to the keys and pushed them under one by one. Almost immediately Helen was trying them in the door.

"This is it!" she said, and the door inched open as Sam tried to get out of the way.

In another half a minute Sam was free. They went to the other door and tried the other keys.

"This is the one! I remember the shape."

In a trice the door was open, and they were looking at the lady from the train. She, like Sam, was tied to a chair, only much tighter, and she was well gagged with a torn up pillow case. Moments later she was free.

"I am most grateful, Sam Johnson – and you, little girl."

"This is Helen," said Sam.

"I am Miss Baxter – Sam and I met on the train coming from London. I am most grateful for your swift action." She stood up, none the worse for her ordeal. (Sam suspected that she was actually refreshed by it.) "But now we must catch the convict!"

Without further fuss, she marched down the stairs, grabbed her umbrella from the floor with a cry of "Ah-ha!" and almost ran out of the cottage and round to the front. Sam and Helen hurried to keep up with her, and Sam spoke quickly as they rushed towards her car.

"Please don't tell the police my uncle had anything to do with it," he panted. "Just tell them the man stole my uncle's car."

Miss Baxter stopped dead in her tracks.

"Is Mr Black your *uncle*, then?" she said sharply. "I felt sure you told me he was a *criminal psychologist*."

"I was lying," said Sam, nearly running into her. "He's my uncle, and he really hasn't done anything wrong, and if he could be let off, I'm sure he'd never do anything stupid again, and—"

Miss Baxter turned and continued rapidly towards her car, which looked too tall, as if it might fall over on sharp bends.

"Jump in, children!" she sang, brightly.

They jumped in, with Sam wondering if she'd heard anything he'd said.

Miss Baxter started the engine, forced it into first gear, revved up hard and released the clutch. The engine roared, the car pounced forward like a springing tiger, and Sam and Helen fell over in the back.

"I don't drive much these days," Miss Baxter murmured. She took her eyes off the road to look back at them and smile.

With the engine screaming, she raced the car down the hill in first gear, and at forty miles an hour changed into second. They went straight out on to the main road, heading towards the village. Each time the engine's screams became unbearable, Miss Baxter changed up another gear.

"One has to use the gears for *maximum acceleration*," she explained, raising her voice to a screech to compete with the engine.

By the time they were out of sight of the cottage, they were travelling at eighty miles an hour, and the first real bend was approaching.

"I don't like bends," she shouted.

Helen and Sam clung to the backs of the front seats in horror as she changed down into third, which jolted the car back down to sixty. Miss Baxter aimed the car at the curve.

"You need to be in a low gear so that you can accelerate out of them," she carolled.

The car threw itself into the curve like a suicide machine. Miss Baxter's foot was already flat on the floor, and there was no acceleration left in the tortured engine.

Luckily, there was nothing coming the other way, and the car lurched round the bend on the wrong side of the road. With metal complaining and tyres squealing, Sam and Helen were compressed into the side of the upholstery. Somehow the car squeezed round, and they were catapulted back in the opposite direction as the road straightened out again.

"That one wasn't so bad, after all," murmured Miss Baxter.

The rest of the journey to the village was of similar nightmarish quality. The hump back bridge was the worst, because it was only when they were actually in the air that Miss Baxter realised there was a sharp bend immediately after it. By a miracle, there was a farm entrance opposite, which Miss Baxter seemed to think was a normal requirement for hump back bridges. They landed in the farmyard, did a handbrake turn on the gravel, and came out again without stopping.

"Dash!" said Miss Baxter. "We wasted a few precious seconds doing that!"

It was Sam who dared to ask the inevitable question.

"We're not trying to catch the men ourselves, are we?" he said. "They must be miles ahead of us."

"I would if I were younger," she said. "I could drive much faster, then."

Helen and Sam exchanged horrified glances and sank back in their seats.

As they approached the village, Sam noticed a lone figure in the middle of a field nearby. It was a man, shoulders bent, and he was carrying a suitcase and plodding doggedly across country in the rough direction of Drift Hill.

"It's Uncle Black!" Sam thought, and was about to shout it, but realised that Miss Baxter might take her eyes off the road to look. He grinned as he realised what it meant. It meant that his uncle had seen sense. He had done what Sam had suggested. And it meant that Charlie Fenwick was on his own.

When they skidded to a halt outside the police station, Miss Baxter was still smiling and very cool, and Sam and Helen were very hot and very relieved. As they rushed inside, Sam quickly told Miss Baxter what he had seen, and immediately started worrying about what she would tell the police. Had she heard him? Did she understand?

Miss Baxter shouted at the man in charge of the desk.

"You must apprehend an escaped convict!" She rapped her umbrella on the floor. "Charlie Fenwick is his name. The man who escaped from the open prison. He's driving towards Carlisle."

At the sound of these words, the machinery of the law jerked into forward motion. There were immediate telephone calls; detailed descriptions; more calls; more questions. It was only when Miss Baxter started to make a formal statement that Sam realised she was even better at telling lies than he was. She invented a story about her friend Mr Jeremy Black being away for the day on a hike, and how she'd been to his cottage to look after it, and how the convict had appeared and tied her up and taken Mr Black's car.

"And almost immediately *these children from the farm*, who were passing the cottage, heard my cries for help, and rescued me."

Sam and Helen stared open-mouthed as Miss Baxter's lies

grew blacker and blacker. They took care to nod obediently each time the sergeant turned to them for confirmation of the story.

At the end, Sam said quietly, "And there's a brooch in the car that belongs to me. Can you get it back, please? It's important, and we don't want that nasty man to lose it."

The desk sergeant wrote it down, and winked at Sam.

"Family heirloom, eh?" he said. "We'll see what we can do." He tidied his papers. "Now – we'll have to get you children back home."

"I'll take them back," said Miss Baxter. Her eyes lit up at the thought of another drive.

The sergeant noticed the look of horror that flickered for a moment across Sam's and Helen's features.

"No, ma'am, that's all right. You live in Carlisle. It's out of your way to go back again. I'm sure the children would enjoy a ride in a nice police car."

"Oh, yes!"

"Yes, please!"

"Well, I am feeling rather tired," admitted Miss Baxter. "I've missed my afternoon nap, as well, so perhaps it will be better if I go straight home. I can see them again another time." She thanked the children again for rescuing her, and said goodbye.

Sam and Helen sat in luxury in a big quiet police car and were driven back to the farm. They noticed that it took the police car twice as long to do the journey as it had taken Miss Baxter.

Helen's mother came to the door to greet them as the police car bounced along the bumpy drive, and her father came in from the fields to see what was happening.

The police car departed, leaving Sam and Helen to recount the version of events that Miss Baxter had made up.

"Well, where's Mr Black, then?" said Mrs Wallace. "It's

funny for him to go on a hike, of all people."

"We don't know, exactly," said Helen, truthfully.

"Well, young man, you'd better stay with us until we know something more," said Mrs Wallace, turning to Sam. "You'd probably enjoy that, wouldn't you?"

"Yes, *please. Thank you.*"

"I'm sure Helen and Jimmy will enjoy it, too," said her husband.

"Yes, ra-ther!" said Helen and Jimmy.

"We must see about collecting your things from the cottage," said Mrs Wallace.

Helen and Sam exchanged anxious glances. Then they chorused, "We'll get them!" and raced outside before anyone could suggest a different idea.

When they had made sure no one had followed them, they climbed into the hay loft. Sam's belongings were just where they had left them.

"Let's have another look at the spaceship before we go back!" said Helen.

She scrambled under the straw where she had hidden it. Suddenly, her whole body registered panic as she started throwing straw in all directions.

"It's gone!" she said. Her heart was struck with horror. "Someone's taken it!"

CHAPTER FIFTEEN

The Docking

"The movement of the Mother Ship has stopped," said Lam. "It has passed within a thousand kilometres of us, but now it lies a thousand kilometres away in a different direction entirely. In fact, almost the opposite direction."

"But a thousand kilometres to us is only half a kilometre to the giant," said Zambel. "From the giant's point of view, it is not very far at all."

"I think perhaps someone should venture outside and try to see our situation," suggested Mogon. "We have been sitting in the darkness now for more than a planet-day. Apart from the low rumbling vibration, the rest of the time there is nothing."

"I still think it is too risky," said Zambel. "I suspect that we are enclosed inside some compartment or pocket. If one of us is outside when a giant decides to move the capsule – what hope is there of ever finding him again?"

"None," said Lam. "Without the Mother Ship we have only minimal bio-computing power. If we had the Mother Ship we would be linked into all the information we needed. And it is also quite possible that by now the main bio-computer has finished analysing the language of the planet."

"If it has," said Zambel, "that would solve a lot of problems for us. We still have no gold for catalysing the fuel process, and we still have no copper for the secondary drive accelerator. To get those, we will have to communicate directly with the giant."

Mogon shrugged.

"But all this is pure speculation if we can't get back to the

Mother Ship at all. Without it we are weak and helpless."

"With it," added Lam, "we are rich and powerful."

"I presume that the sealed unit is still sealed?"

"Yes, Zambel. No unnatural light has fallen on the Ark whatsoever. The Ark is still sealed and our people and our ecological systems are still safe. I only wish I knew for how much longer."

"Something is happening," said Lam.

Zambel and Mogon felt the movement, too. They came to the bio-screen.

Suddenly, bright sunlight sparkled through the diamond windows and glittered on the walls and equipment inside. They heard a low booming noise like the sound of a distant rumble of thunder. Then, just as suddenly, it was dark again.

Now there was the sickening motion that they had all grown used to. The capsule rocked backwards and forwards, up and down in the black world around them.

Lam, his eyes on the bio-screen, called out.

"The Ark is coming closer – or rather, we must be getting closer to the Ark."

"What is the rate of approach?"

"Twenty thousand kilometres per hour; now slowing slightly to ten thousand."

"Direction?"

"Our compass position remains the same. We are moving directly towards it."

For the first time in many hours, the Zargans allowed themselves room for hope.

"The closer we get," said Mogon, "the higher we can raise our hopes."

They continued to stare at the bio-screen as Lam read out the constantly changing statistics. Their pleasure and relief increased with each passing minute.

"We are now within one hundred and fifty kilometres."

"Nothing to a giant," said Mogon.

"Now the compass bearing is changing rapidly."

"No wonder I am feeling sick."

"Fifty kilometres. . . Forty. . . Twenty. . . Ten. . . Five. . . One. . ."

Suddenly dim light filtered through the windows and a great cheer went up inside.

"I can see out!" said Zambel. "We are inside a building – a gloomy building."

Then the light went off again, then on, then off, then on once more. This time it was Mogon who called from another porthole, "I can see her! The Ark is here!"

Lam left the bio-screen and joined them at the windows.

"Only the top is exposed, but look!" Mogon pointed.

They looked.

They were being docked.

CHAPTER SIXTEEN

The Flight

"It can't have gone!" said Sam. "It can't have! You must have left it somewhere else!"

Helen's face was reddening as she scattered straw in every direction.

"I know where I put it! I put it just here – and it's gone!"

Sam helped her, flinging the heaps of straw everywhere to see if their beloved metal cigar was anywhere underneath.

"What about your mum or dad – could they have taken it?"

"They would have said something. They wouldn't just take it away."

"What about Jimmy?"

"It's far too heavy. He couldn't possibly have moved it down the ladder."

"Well, where is it, then?"

"I don't know!" Helen screamed, vermilion by now. "Oh, it's such a rotten end! Someone's been in here and taken it away, just as you said they would. They must have seen all the emeralds. It's probably in London by now, being sold for thousands of pounds."

"It was probably just green glass, not emeralds," said Sam. It was all he could think of to say, but somehow it didn't seem to make things any better.

They searched all round inside the barn, but found nothing.

"Do you think it could have taken off?" said Sam.

"It wouldn't take off without the little spaceship," said Helen. "They wouldn't be so horrible."

Sam wanted to laugh.

"What do you mean, they wouldn't be so horrible? It's a

spaceship, Helen. It came from outer space. The little ship is probably just a sort of scouting vehicle. If it didn't come back after two or three days, perhaps they agreed that they'd have to take off and leave it here."

Helen gave up looking and sat down heavily on a pile of rope.

"So now we'll get the brooch back from the police, and we'll have to write on a little piece of paper 'Sorry, but you've just missed your spaceship'."

Sam smiled wryly, but still couldn't laugh.

"We'll never find out what *really* happened to it," Helen went on. "If someone's stolen it, *they'll* never tell anyone."

Sam stood up.

"Let's take the suitcases into the house. Perhaps your mum and dad know something but just forgot to tell us in all the other excitement."

"Okay," said Helen. There was no energy in her voice. She dragged herself to her feet and slowly helped Sam to manoeuvre his belongings down the ladder.

"It's my fault," she said.

"Of course it's not."

"It is. You gave the spaceship to me when your uncle was chasing you, and that's the last time you saw it. It *must* be my fault if it's gone now, mustn't it?"

"Well, that's one each, then," said Sam. "It was me that lost the little one." He sighed. "And I came back last night, as well – for my torch. I could have looked at it, but I was surprised to see you asleep in here. I didn't want to disturb you, then. Perhaps it had already gone."

Helen cheered up a bit as she remembered the events of the day before.

"I watched your uncle trying to catch you. It was quite funny, really. I got back safely with the spaceship, then waited in my room in case you signalled, but of course you didn't have your torch. So I crept down here to look at the spaceship again. I wanted to be here if you came back with the little one, so that we could join them up again. Thanks for the note, by the way."

"That's okay. It was just to let you know where I was."

Slowly, they started carrying Sam's luggage out of the barn towards the house.

"By the way," said Sam, "I didn't say thanks for rescuing me."

"Oh, that was easy. I just watched the cottage all morning. I saw the other car drive up, and later you came running out like mad. "Then," – her face imitated her own look of horror – "I saw your uncle driving along the road. I wanted you to escape, but it was hopeless, wasn't it? He caught you, and there was nothing I could do about it."

"That was bad luck."

"I knew you'd need me sooner or later, so I stalked back to the cottage to wait until everyone had gone. Then my idiot brother Jimmy suddenly dug me in the back and I nearly died of fright! I thought I'd been caught by your uncle! The little nuisance followed me, even though I warned him to keep away. I told him to get home without being seen, or Old Shoutbum would lock him up!"

They reached the farmhouse, where Helen's father helped them in with the cases.

"That was quick!" said Mrs Wallace. "You haven't been all the way to Drift Hill and back already, surely?"

"We ran," said Sam, and he and Helen laughed.

Mrs Wallace shook her head sadly, the way mothers do, and busied herself round the house.

"Have you or Dad found anything in the hay loft today?" Helen asked casually.

"What sort of thing?"

"Oh, it's just a toy spaceship that Sam brought down yesterday. It's disappeared."

"No, I've seen nothing."

146

They went upstairs. Helen's room seemed dull now that they didn't have dead ants and space messages to look at under the microscope. They sat down and tried to think what they could do.

Then the doorbell rang. Mrs Wallace answered it, but the children could only hear her side of the conversation.

"Yes? Oh – oh, good. Really? That was quick. Well, I never. The what? Oh – I see. I'll tell him. Thank you. All right, then. Goodbye."

Mrs Wallace came upstairs.

"That was the police. The escaped convict has been caught. The police wanted me to tell you both that they're very grateful for all your help. They also said something about a brooch. . ."

"Yes?" said Sam. He brightened up for the first time in a long while. "Have they found it?"

"No," said Mrs Wallace. "The sergeant said to tell you that they searched the car and the man's belongings, but it's nowhere to be found."

Sam and Helen were devastated. Back in Helen's room, they hung their heads and thought of all the fun they'd had finding the real, live spaceships. They'd been through trouble and danger as well, to help the little people from another planet. But now it seemed as if it had all been for nothing.

All was lost. No matter how wild their imagination, they couldn't see any way of saving the situation. There was no possibility that either the brooch or the big spaceship would ever be seen again. Except, if the big spaceship had been stolen, perhaps the little people would come swarming out and take revenge on the thieves. Or perhaps they would stop being friendly little people and take over the whole planet. They would be more successful than ants; more voracious than locusts; more dangerous than the tsetse fly. They would conquer the world. Men would become their slaves. . .

It was only when they had reached this astounding conclusion that they noticed Jimmy standing in the doorway.

"Where have you been?" said Helen, feeling cross.

"I've got a secret," said Jimmy.

"Well, we don't want to hear it," said Helen. "And anyway, it won't be a secret any more if you tell us."

"It's a special secret."

Helen let out the deep sigh of a long-suffering sister.

"Oh, go on, then – what is it?"

Jimmy looked from one to the other, pleased with himself.

"I know where the spaceship is," he said.

Helen glanced up quickly. Then her face fell again as she realised he'd probably been poking around in the straw while she'd been watching the cottage for signs of Sam.

"Well, hard luck, it's not there any more," she said. "It's been stolen."

"It hasn't," said Jimmy.

"Yes it has. We've just looked ten minutes ago."

"It hasn't," said Jimmy. "I know where it is."

Suddenly, Helen and Sam were on their feet.

"What do you mean?"

"Where is it?"

Jimmy gestured for them to follow him. He led them out of the house, across a field and through a hedge, all in the opposite direction from Drift Hill. In the next field they saw it. It was sitting in the grass, out of sight of any buildings, glistening in the late afternoon sunshine.

"Jimmy! You are clever! How did you find it?"

Jimmy beamed.

"It was in the hay loft where you left it," he said. "I knew it was there, cos I watched you put it in."

"This is incredible," said Helen. "Jimmy – how did it get *here*? You can't have carried it yourself – it's far too heavy – and you couldn't possibly have got it down that steep

148

ladder without someone helping."

"It *flew* here," said Jimmy.

Helen and Sam stared. He was joking. Surely, he was joking.

"Don't be silly."

"It *did* fly here," Jimmy said firmly. "I followed it."

Now they stared at him open-mouthed.

"Well? Were you just looking at it when it suddenly flew here, or what?"

"Did you see it from the house?"

"Did you see it from the yard?"

"Where were you?"

"What happened?"

Jimmy didn't seem to understand their impatience.

"It was easy," he said. Then he started laughing and jumping up and down.

"For heaven's sake, keep still, and tell us!" screamed Helen.

"It flew here when I put the brooch in!" shouted Jimmy.

CHAPTER SEVENTEEN

The Departure

"We have been placed in correct docking position," said Lam. "I am now locking into place."

"We must take full readings of our situation here. We have been imperilled for long enough. If we are inside a building we must leave it as soon as possible."

"I am running initialisation checks," said Lam. "Is it our giant who brought us here?"

"No," said Mogon, who was carrying out a detailed visual survey. "It is a smaller giant. Possibly one of the giants that was with our giant when we first saw them."

"Then our message worked," said Zambel. "We owe a great debt to these friendly creatures."

"Their intelligence is more than we could have hoped for," said Mogon. "To find our Ark at such a great distance, and to bring it safely back – that is a miracle."

Lam became floppy with excitement.

"Zambel! The Ark bio-computers have completed their analysis of the planet's languages. The language in most use on radio waves in this area has been selected, and an audio representation of it compiled. The frequency is far too low for us to detect with our own ears, and the speed of their speech is twenty times slower than ours."

"What are the recommendations?"

"The bio-computer recommends that we establish a device, working through one of the existing external air channels, through which sound from the bio-computer translation unit can be transmitted and received."

"Does it give a specification?"

"Yes. A full specification is here. It can be constructed in a very short time."

"Excellent. Mogon and I shall commence work immediately. What does the environmental report tell us?"

"We are inside a building, but with free access to the outside through a door. I would suggest that we will be safer in the open air, where we can leave all systems on emergency standby for take-off. If we stay in the building, the door may be shut, and our escape route cut off."

"Then do it now."

"We are immersed in flammable material inside a flammable building. I recommend the use of anti-gravity propulsion for safety."

"Very well."

Lam passed a hand over the pulse pad several times.

"Take care to avoid the little giant," said Zambel. "And move slowly enough for it to follow us. We will then be able to set up our communications."

Lam nodded.

Slowly, the spacecraft rose. Taking care not to lose the giant, which was following at its incredibly slow rate, Lam steered their home through the open doorway and out into the bright sunlight of the planet.

"What do you mean, when you put the *brooch* in?" said Helen. "Where did you get the brooch *from?*"

"From Old Shoutbum's car," said Jimmy. "I took it when he wasn't looking."

"Jimmy, you're brilliant!" Helen's face started to radiate extreme happiness, while Sam was still staring open-mouthed at Jimmy's startling revelations.

"How did you know it was there?" said Sam.

"I didn't," said Jimmy. "I just looked."

Slowly, by a difficult series of questions and answers, Jimmy's story unfolded. He had been excluded from their adventure, but he had followed them and listened whenever he could. When Helen had returned with the big spaceship and sworn him to secrecy, he discovered that they still hadn't found the brooch, and that Sam would make another attempt that night.

Jimmy had then followed Helen on her devious route to the cottage to wait to rescue Sam, but had made the mistake of tapping her on the shoulder for a joke. As a result he'd been sent away for being naughty. But on his way back round the house he'd seen the car. Sam and Helen hadn't looked in the car, so Jimmy would look in the car. And there in the glove compartment he had found the brooch.

His pride and pleasure as he ran down the hill with it clutched in his hand were unbounded. And when he found that the little brooch fitted into the slot on the spaceship – just like the picture said it would – he was overjoyed. And then, when it *flew*. . .!

It was as the three children were holding hands and doing a little dance round the spaceship that they heard the voice. It was thin and metallic, but it was nevertheless a voice.

"This is the BBC," it said. "This is the BBC."

"Someone's left a radio on," said Sam.

"No, listen!" said Helen. "It's coming from the spaceship!"

They stopped dancing and knelt down close to the big metal cigar.

"This is the BBC," it said, over and over again.

"Hello!" said Sam. "Hello!"

"It is now ten minutes past eight!" said the spaceship.

"You're two minutes fast," said Sam, looking at his watch.

"Thank you," said the spaceship.

"Who are you?" said Sam.

"We are from the planet Zarg, two thousand light-years away from your planet, Earth."

"How do you know our planet is called Earth, and how can you speak our language?" asked Helen.

"The computers on board our mother ship have been absorbing your radio broadcasts on the clearest frequencies. They have analysed the signals, converted them to sound-pulses using millions of different formulae, and carried out millions of comparisons with sound-pulses issuing from the handful of humans we have encountered on the planet. Eventually, a match was found. In this way we have managed to calculate the method by which you convert your radio signals to sound. Does that answer your question?"

"Yes, thank you," said Helen, slightly overwhelmed. She turned quietly to Sam. "Remind me not to ask any more technical questions, will you?"

"I am Zambel," said the voice. "My two colleagues are Mogon and Lam. What is the name of the human who wrote the messages to us?"

"Sam Johnson."

"And who is the little one who docked our capsule into the mother ship?"

"Jimmy Wallace," said Jimmy proudly.

"Who is the third one?"

"Helen Wallace."

"We couldn't have done any of it without Helen," said Sam. "She carried the mother ship to safety."

"First of all," said Zambel, "I wish to thank you all from the bottom of our hearts for what you have done. We became accidentally separated from the Ark when we landed. In our terms, we were separated from it by twelve thousand kilometres. We had no chance of getting back to it, under the circumstances. Thanks only to you, we have succeeded."

"We wanted to," said Sam. "We wanted to help you."

"Why are you here on our planet, and why have you come so far?" said Helen.

153

"Our planet Zarg, five thousand years ago, began to overheat. Our government decided that for Zargankind to survive, we would have to build an ark.

"But we would build as many arks as we could. As long as Zargans were alive on Zarg, more arks would be built. The ark you are looking at now is the ninety-seventh ark to leave our planet. Conditions were getting bad when we departed. We do not believe that many more could have been built after that. . .

"Each ark contains a sealed biosphere, perfectly balanced to sustain a Zargan environment until the end of time. Our unit contains the descendants, hundreds of generations further on, of those Zargans who first set out from our planet five thousand years ago.

"Some Zargans are trained to control the spaceship. When the life of one of the three commanders comes to an end, a new commander is released through a series of one-way air-locks to join the other two in the control capsule – the little spaceship that you found."

"We thought it was a brooch!" said Jimmy.

"Each ark was assigned four hundred square degrees of space in which to look for new worlds to live on. Our generations in Ark Ninety-seven have been looking for a suitable planet for all this time. Unfortunately, all the best planets are already inhabited. It is not our policy to dominate a planet, but to find one where life has not yet begun – so that our ecology will be exactly as it was on Zarg, without change."

By this time the three children were sitting down, clustered in a tight circle around the strange metallic object that lay in the grass in the field.

"Aren't you getting tired of looking?" asked Sam.

"The only existence we know is our life in the sealed unit, or – for a few lucky ones – the life of a commander. When we find the planet we are seeking, then we shall adapt and adjust. Not before."

"Why did you land on Earth?" Helen asked again.

"Our spaceship is driven by the pure energy of which atoms are made – what you would call nuclear power, but controlled in a way that we have developed over hundreds of centuries. You need not fear. You are not in danger of exposure to radiation.

"We use the element gold as a key catalyst in this process. We have landed here because we do not have sufficient gold on board to take us to the next planetary system. This is where we need your help again."

"I've got a gold bracelet," said Helen.

"May we use it? We do not need a large amount. A few micrograms."

"You can have it all if you like."

"That will not be necessary."

Helen slipped off her bracelet and placed it on top of the spaceship, near the control capsule.

"We are indebted to you," said Zambel.

The children saw nothing happening, but half a minute later Zambel's voice was heard again.

"Thank you. You may take it back now."

"You can't have done it already!"

"In your terms, Helen, it took us ten minutes. We have estimated that our perception of time is twenty times faster than yours. It has only taken me *one* of your seconds to say this, but it will take you *twenty* of your seconds to listen to it. I'm afraid *we* have to wait a lot of our time between each communication!"

"I see."

"That is also why it is difficult to see us. We move five times faster than your red horses – or ants, should I say!"

"We'd love to see you – can we, please?"

"By the time you have finished hearing my reply, Lam will be standing outside the diamond window nearest to Jimmy."

Three eager pairs of eyes jostled for the best position to see a Zargan at last. In front of the little window they could just make out the tiny, tiny speck, no taller than an ant, and as thin as a thread of cotton. It was far too small for them to discern the three arms and legs they had seen in the drawing. Neither did they see it move, but suddenly it was gone.

"We also need copper," said Zambel. "Do you have any? We need to repair one of our machines."

"There are lots of things like that in the barn," said Helen. "I'll go and find some."

Helen returned with a long length of copper pipe and rested it carefully on top of the spaceship as before.

Shortly afterwards, Zambel thanked her. Helen tossed the pipe to one side, but Sam rescued it and looked at it closely.

"It's just got a tiny gouge in it," he said. "Is that really all you needed? I can't believe you had to go to all that trouble to land on Earth just for that little bit."

"It's only a little bit to you, Sam. In our terms we have taken, in fact, several tons."

"But how could you take it so quickly?"

"You are asking me to reveal the secrets of centuries of technological development in a few minutes? I'm sorry, but it's not possible. Also, because of our size, we have physical forces working for us at atomic level that you giants would find very difficult to harness."

"Do you know where you'll be going to next?" said Helen.

"Our journey will continue in the same direction that we have followed for the last five thousand years."

"Why don't you try Mars?" said Jimmy suddenly. "There's no one living there at the moment."

"That is an excellent suggestion, Jimmy. It is on the other side of the sun, and we are going in that direction. We will look at it on the way."

"How many Zargans are on board your ship?" asked Sam.

"Approximately half a million."

Sam whistled.

"You can't have as many as that in such a small thing!"

"But we have. In your terms it is a city one and a half kilometres long, but it is a city with many layers, one above the other, each one with its own characteristics. By working hard, Zargans can earn the right to visit a different level. But speaking of working hard, you must now tell us if there is anything we can do for you? We owe our very existence to your hard work."

The three children thought carefully, but couldn't think of anything that such small creatures could do for them. Sam wanted his own private spaceship, Helen wanted a pony of her own, and Jimmy wanted an electric train set.

"We cannot help you with those things," said Zambel. "But Lam and Mogon have come up with an idea. When do your birthdays occur?"

The three children gave their birth dates eagerly. Would the Zargans send them a present each? It seemed impossible.

"Good," said Zambel. "This is how we have decided to reward you. When we leave the Earth and gather speed, we shall shepherd three bands of particles into elliptical orbits round your sun – one band of particles for each of you. Lam will calculate their orbits so that the Earth passes through them on each of your birthdays. You will then have your very own meteor shower every year on your birthday. Before the first one happens, however, you must write to the Royal Astronomical Society and all the astronomical periodicals and official bodies and *predict* the appearance of the meteor showers on those dates. You will then have the right to name them officially as the Sam Johnson, the Helen Wallace and the Jimmy Wallace displays respectively!"

"Oh, thank you, thank you! That'll be wonderful!"

The three of them jumped up and down like Jimmy, and cheered.

"We'll be famous!"

"Hooray!"

The darkness was falling rapidly now as the sun disappeared behind the hills. The tinny voice spoke for the last time.

"It is dark and we must leave you now. If we do settle on Mars, we shall always watch this place. If you ever need our help, we will see your signal. And I hope that when each of you has a birthday, you will remember us."

"We will!"

"We'll always remember you!"

The three human children stood back a little way and watched, proud and excited, as the beautiful metal cigar, with its diamonds and emeralds sparkling, started to move.

They all heard the hiss of rushing air. They saw in the darkness the tiny laser beams of the Zargans' Ark rising above their heads, higher and higher into the night. When it was a long way up, bright streamers of light suddenly appeared beneath its base, wavering and shimmering with energy. The noise of compressed air was abruptly shut off, and silence cascaded down to their ears. Soundlessly, the spaceship rose up into the black sky on a column of pink and green light.

Without a word, they stood and watched it fade into the stars.

CHAPTER EIGHTEEN

The End

Later that evening, a light came on in Drift Hill Cottage and Sam and Helen walked up the fell to call on a subdued Uncle Black. Sam reassured him that the police knew nothing of his involvement, and his uncle seemed grateful. Sam said that he had been invited to stay at the farm, and Uncle Black raised no objection.

Back at the farm, Sam and Helen sat down and started writing letters. They wrote letters to the Royal Astronomical Society; Jodrell Bank Observatory; the Royal Observatory; a letter to the BBC for *Sky at Night*; and letters to every newspaper and Astronomical Society they could find.

Mr Wallace, despite his amusement at their efforts, humoured them and took them into the village shop the following day so that they could look up the addresses in the library. While they were in the village, they telephoned national newspapers and asked for the addresses of other places they'd heard of, and in the process managed to get addresses for lots of other people and places they hadn't heard of.

It was a Herculean effort, and they sent off thirty letters in all. After an agonising delay of several days, they received a few replies.

Some of the replies said, "The Editor thanks you for your communication, which is receiving attention." One or two of the observatories wrote back, asking them to specify the area of sky in which the meteor showers would appear, and asking on what evidence and observations the predictions had been made? One person telephoned, but as soon as he found out that Sam Johnson, Helen Wallace and Jimmy Wallace were only *children* who didn't even possess a telescope, he promptly told them to stop wasting people's time with things they knew nothing about.

As the rest of Sam's three weeks in Cumbria came to an end, the memory and excitement of the first few days seemed like a funny dream. Whenever they weakened for a moment and thought that perhaps it *was* all a dream, Sam would take out the little piece of paper from his travelling clock and they would look at it under the microscope. The drawings were there, just as they remembered them.

They showed the drawings to Mr and Mrs Wallace when they had time to look at them. But they had both laughed at the story of the spaceship that had split in half, and told the children they were very clever to be able to make drawings as tiny as that. "Had they used a needle?" they had asked, then chuckled and lost interest.

Later, Helen had a brainwave and looked at her bracelet under the microscope. There it was, a little neat hole in the gold, but that was all: just a neat hole.

The ants they collected had disappeared long ago because they hadn't looked after them. A visit to the outbuilding at Drift Hill Cottage revealed no further supply of bodies – the others had been blown away, or eaten, or collected by the other ants.

"I knew no one would believe us," said Sam. "That's the trouble when you keep a secret like that. No one believes you."

"Never mind," said Helen. "We know it really happened, and that's all that matters, really, isn't it? And Jimmy knows as well."

"We didn't even *think* to take any photographs."

"They wouldn't have done any good. People would just have looked at them and said they were photographs of toys."

"No one at school is going to believe it. And everyone else thinks we're mad already, including your parents and every newspaper and observatory in the country."

"Of course. I bet when you used to read about people seeing flying saucers, you thought they were mad."

"But I always *wanted* to believe in them," said Sam. "And now that I *do*, I can't convince anyone else."

Miss Baxter had written, asking how the children were feeling after their terrible ordeal. Sam and Helen thought she meant the journey in her car, but she didn't. She apologised for not coming to see Sam, but she had been very busy. When was Sam going back? She had to go to London herself soon. Perhaps they could travel together?

Sam groaned at the thought.

The day for his departure arrived, and he visited Uncle Black to say goodbye. He promised his sorry-looking uncle that he would never tell anyone what really happened. He would tell his parents how well he had been looked after. Uncle Black produced a very relieved smile and agreed that, in return, he would say nothing about the letter that Sam had hidden from his parents.

"I was a fool," said Uncle Black. "I made a stupid promise to an old acquaintance. I was sorry as soon as I did it."

They were friends again, and his uncle shook hands and bade him a fond farewell.

Sam said goodbye to Mr and Mrs Wallace, who had taken him to the station, and thanked them for everything. He said goodbye to Jimmy and thanked him for being so brilliant for thinking of looking in Uncle Black's car. Finally, he said goodbye to Helen. He wanted to tell her how much he liked her, but didn't really know how to say it.

"It's my birthday first," he said at last. "In a month's time. Don't forget to watch the sky all night for me. You'll get a better view up here."

"I'll be watching," said Helen. Her eyes were bright and

she was smiling.

Sam turned and climbed on to the train and saw with a sinking heart that Miss Baxter was hurrying up the platform towards him. Unfortunately, Miss Baxter had kept in close touch with the Wallaces, and knew which train he was catching.

Sam waved and waved until the diminishing figures on the platform had disappeared completely. He closed the window and sat down to face Miss Baxter's inquisition.

It began immediately.

"There are one or two questions I would like you to answer," she said.

Sam took a deep breath. He wasn't in the mood for telling lies.

"You have been most untruthful," she said. "I asked you some questions on the way to Carlisle on the train. You told me that you lived in a cave in the Himalayas, which was quite ridiculous, of course. I have since made enquiries and discovered your real address. What do you have to say about it?"

Sam didn't have anything to say about it. He wanted to read his new book, *The Galaxy of Fear*.

"Nothing. I see," said Miss Baxter. "Silence is the surest sign of guilt."

Sam looked longingly at his book, then not at all longingly at Miss Baxter.

"I rescued you," he said, simply.

Miss Baxter smiled.

"Ah, yes. And I am most grateful. Most grateful. But what I am saying is this: you told me a pack of lies on the way to Carlisle. You told me that you were going to be seen by a 'criminal psychologist' called Jeremy Black. Now – I never had the chance to meet this Mr Black – but I since discovered, of course, that he was your uncle, hiding the escaped convict, Charlie Fenwick, at the cottage. Isn't that true?"

"Yes," said Sam. It was easier to tell the truth. "But you must never tell anyone, because he didn't really mean it. He thought he was helping an old friend. He didn't realise how stupid it was until I arrived and messed it all up."

"He is not, then, a criminal psychologist in his spare time?"

"No," said Sam.

"And your father is not a millionaire hermit?"

"No," said Sam.

"And your mother – didn't really marry a Swedish Prince?"

"No."

"And doesn't live in Brazil?"

"No."

Miss Baxter allowed a little smile to play on her lips.

"So is it true that on the train coming up, *everything* you told me was a *lie*?"

"Yes," said Sam.

"Since you are now telling me the truth – because I have checked all the points on which you have just been questioned – does this mean that you have now forsaken the *silly* path of telling lies?"

"Yes," said Sam.

"Good!" Miss Baxter clapped her hands gently together and relaxed back in her seat. "Now – I want to know the *whole* story of this unfortunate incident with your uncle. I shan't repeat it elsewhere. Just tell me what happened when you arrived."

"The house was locked and I slept in the garden," said Sam.

Miss Baxter's face, which had just risen, fell again.

"I want the *truth!*" she said.

"That is the truth, honestly," said Sam.

Miss Baxter frowned and looked Sam straight in the eye.

163

"Is that really the truth, Sam Johnson?" she said.

It was not pleasant, but he looked Miss Baxter in the eye.

"Yes," he said.

"Very well. It seems a strange welcome from an uncle, but. . . I shall accept for the moment that you are telling me the truth. What happened next?"

"I saw a UFO," said Sam.

"A – what? – a UFO? – don't tell me, I have an excellent memory – an Unidentified Flying Object?"

"Yes," said Sam.

She glanced at the cover of Sam's book.

"I understand they are seen quite frequently by people with. . . peculiar imaginations."

As she made herself more comfortable in her seat, Sam glared at her.

"It was a *real* one," he said.

"What do you mean, little boy – a *real* one?"

"A real *spaceship*," said Sam.

A look of impatience crossed Miss Baxter's brow.

"I think," she began – "that we have traversed that naughty little boundary into fantasy again. I am interested to know the *truth* of your adventure with your uncle. Please tell me again, without fabrication. *Lying* is such a horrible habit."

"*You lied*," said Sam accusingly.

"Me?" squeaked Miss Baxter, shocked at the thought. "I *never* tell lies."

"You lied to the police," Sam reminded her.

"Oh, *that* – that was to protect your uncle, dear boy." She squirmed in her seat. "That doesn't count."

"Well," said Sam, "it *was* a real spaceship. It had split into two. We found one half, and they shot some ants with bows and arrows, and we talked to the people inside by drawing pictures. They were only one millimetre high, but they drew some pictures for us and told us where to find their big spaceship. Then we found it, and—"

164

"*STOP!*" cried Miss Baxter. "Unless you *desist* from this habitual tendency to *fantasise*, I have no wish to listen to any more."

"It's *true!*" said Sam. "You'll see."

"Is that your last word?"

"Yes."

"Then I have no more to say. I thought that *at last* you had learned to be *truthful*, but it seems that I am mistaken."

"It's *true*—" Sam began again, but noted the look of annoyance and exasperation on Miss Baxter's face.

Then he brightened. It was, of course, the sort of look that would give him a clear hour's uninterrupted reading of *The Galaxy of Fear*.

It was only as the train drew nearer to London that Sam began to realise the enormity of his past crimes. Not showing Aunt Mabel's letter to his parents was the same as lying to them, and he never lied to his parents. It had seemed a harmless prank at the time, to get himself a holiday in Cumbria. Now it loomed large as what it really was – a dangerous, disobedient and stupid thing to do. While he could easily deny any knowledge of receiving the letter, his telephone call from Carlisle station was another matter. . .

He rehearsed his excuses in his mind.

"I realised Uncle Black wasn't there, and I didn't want to worry you. . ."

"I waited for ages. I thought he might have broken down, so I got a taxi. . ."

"I didn't want to spoil your business trip. . ."

"And when I arrived and realised Auntie Mabel wouldn't be there. . ."

By the time Sam reached home, he had rehearsed his innocence so well that he convinced not only himself, but his parents as well. He told them about a lost letter that Auntie Mabel had written, calling the holiday off. He told them about Uncle Black's shock at his arrival, and how he had eventually allowed Sam to stay with his new friends at the farm. Later, he told them the whole story of the spaceship. That was when Mr and Mrs Johnson asked him if he was feeling all right.

When he showed them copies of the letters they had written to the societies and newspapers, and the Zargans' writing on the small piece of paper, they smiled and seemed to take an interest. Secretly, they seemed to be thinking that three weeks without them had caused the balance of his mind to become permanently disturbed.

They treated him strangely after that. His mother made frequent enquiries about his health and well-being, and his father came home with piles of science fiction books and bags of sweets.

Sam wrote to Helen and told her that his parents thought he was mad.

When his birthday arrived at last, Sam asked if he could sleep in the garden to watch for his meteor shower. At first his parents were dead set against the idea. But when Sam started showing (fake) signs of mental distress, his request was granted.

"Why don't you come and see as well?" he pleaded.

"But, Sam. . ."

"You still don't believe it'll happen, do you?"

"We think you had a very exciting holiday, but it's over now. Why don't you just stop kidding yourself and forget about it?"

"Please. . ."

Reluctantly, at dusk, they accompanied him to the blankets that he had laid on polythene sheeting on the grass. All three of them, well wrapped up, lay on their backs looking at the clear black sky of a hundred billion stars.

Unknown to them, in a score of different gardens all over the country, a score of professors and scientists, instead of watching television or reading a book, were also scanning the night sky. Each of them clutched a letter written by three children they had never heard of, and they all hoped in their hearts that something would happen just as their letter said it would.

So when they appeared, thousands of them, those great cascades of meteors, streaming down the sky to wish Sam a Happy Birthday, the whole of mankind knew that he, and Helen and Jimmy Wallace, were the three luckiest children in the world.